I0657009

Martha Louise Rayne

Against Fate

A true story

Martha Louise Rayne

Against Fate
A true story

ISBN/EAN: 9783744748575

Printed in Europe, USA, Canada, Australia, Japan

Cover: Foto ©Andreas Hilbeck / pixelio.de

More available books at **www.hansebooks.com**

A TRUE STORY:

By MRS. M. L. RAYNE.

CHICAGO:
W. B. KEEN, COOKE & CO.
1876.

COPYRIGHT.

A. D. 1876.

Lakeside Press, Chicago.

CONTENTS.

4 CONTENTS.

AGAINST FATE.

CHAPTER I.

OUT INTO THE WORLD.

"How shall it be with her, the tender stranger,
　　Fair-faced and gentle-eyed,
Before whose unstained feet the world's rude highway
　　Stretches so strange and wide?"

GOOD-BYE, Mother! Now don't you fret about me at all. I shall write often and tell you just how I get along. And may be I'll come home at Christmas. You shall have a new dress for a present, if I don't come. I am going to save my money on purpose. Now don't cry, please, there's a dear good mother. It will all come out right."

"I hope it may, Jennie," answered the mother, sadly; "but, oh dear! I've never slept a night

without you under the same roof, and if anything
should happen it would break my heart. It does
seem to me that I shall never have you back
again, the Jennie I see before me. Somehow I
mistrust that woman you are going to. I wish
we knew more about her. She has promised
well, I know, but will she keep her promises?"

"It will not take long to decide that, mother!"

"Yes; and I suppose it will be better than
going into a store; but oh, it does seem as
though I cannot give you up!"

Mrs. Armstrong looked at her daughter, and
it required all the stern discipline of her reserved
nature to keep her from breaking down utterly,
as she parted with her only child, fearing in her
heart, she knew not what evil, poor woman! She
had fallen into the useless habit of looking on
the dark side of everything, which was no very
surprising circumstance, considering that her
blessings all came in disguise; even this precious child, growing from lovely girlhood into
lovelier womanhood, had always been a source
of exquisite sorrow. How to get enough to
clothe her comfortably, to give her even an
ordinary education, to surround her with the

smallest and poorest luxuries — a few of the
many little pleasures which young girls crave —
this had been the end and aim of the mother's
existence. Herself a disappointed woman, she
had struggled hard to gain for Jennie something
of all she had missed. She had tried and failed.
Many nights the mother had lain awake schem-
ing and planning for Jennie, while the girl slept
and found in rosy dreams a compensation for
the day's losses.

"You haven't half enough clothes," continued
Mrs. Armstrong, looking wistfully at the little
red leather trunk on the stoop. "That merino
is worn so thin it didn't make over very well, and
the plush cape looks faded; but the brown rep is
as good as new. That will wear all winter comfortably. Did your father give you any money?"
This last was asked in an eager whisper, with a
wistful glance toward the tall, solemn looking
man who was harnessing a rickety horse into a
more rickety wagon, preparatory to taking his
daughter to the depot.

"No," answered the girl in a low tone,
reddening slowly as she spoke. She hated the
name of money, for it represented to her all

mean and sordid make-shifts! If she could only have a room full of it, she would be happy; but these crumbs from the table — bah!

"Well! here are two dollars," said Mrs. Armstrong, "all I have in the world. Perhaps your father will give you a little more, and you must be careful of it, dear, for I'm sure I don't know where the next is coming from!"

As Jennie had never received a shilling in her life, without a table of instructions added, this caution was unnecessary. She took the money in a thankless sort of way and crushed it into the palm of her cotton glove. She wanted to throw it down, trample upon it and make it feel how lightly she esteemed it, the miserable paltry sum! A very human girl, this one, you see!

But she saw the tearful face of that dear, good mother, who had stood like a wall of defense between her and life ever since she entered it, and now she was going out into the great beautiful world without her! It seemed so ungrateful after all that mother had done.

And sobbing as she had not done since a child, Jennie clung about her mother's neck, kissing and clasping her in a straining embrace. Then she climbed over the high wheel into the old wagon and took her place by her father's side; the gaunt old horse started off, and they were gone!

But the girl looked back with such genuine sorrow for the miserable home she was leaving, it was a wonder she did not share the fate of that tragic woman perpetuated in salt. As she looked she saw through the crystal of her tears, that her mother was hurrying after her, holding out a small book.

"You forgot it, Jennie, dear," she said as she came up almost breathless from the unusual exertion of running. "I found it on the bed where you had overlooked it."

A frown ruffled the low, smooth brow of the girl, and the pretty tremulous lips contracted pettishly, but she took the little volume and squeezed the thin hand of her mother lovingly.

"Read it often, Jennie, dear; you will find peace and comfort there when all else fails. I have marked some comforting words in the Epistle of St. John."

"I hear the train, Mary," interrupted Mr.

Armstrong. "Women never know when to let well enough alone. Get up," said he to his horse; "look out there for the wheel," turning to his wife, and they started on.

"Good-bye, Jennie, darling; be a good girl, and write home often." These were the last homely words of the sorrowing mother.

Jennie soon dried her eyes — the tears of youth are easily exhausted — and began to speculate on the probable events of her journey to Chicago, and the improbable happiness of the bright future that awaited her there. The little book in her lap slid down into the bottom of the wagon and lay there unnoticed. She was thinking of all the fine sights she would see, the money she would have, the books she could read, the dresses she would wear. Her eyes grew bright, her cheeks red, her lips smiled and she sat like an enchanted Hebe beside her taciturn father, and had traveled miles in imagination when they stopped at the dingy depot.

But the mother had gone back to the house — had entered the little, disorderly, ill fitted bedroom now drearily vacant, and had thrown herself on her knees beside the empty bed and with her face buried in her check apron, was fighting a battle to the death !

There were two other girls at the depot waiting for the coming train. They were school mates and companions of Jennie's, and were now looking for her with much solicitude, as the three were going together to seek their fortunes in the city. One had been a teacher of the district school in the next township for the last year, and expected to obtain a situation in the public schools of Chicago at a better remuneration. The other was a bright girl, who had assisted her widowed mother by clerking in the one general store — the place being post office, dry goods shop, and grocery combined. She hoped to realize more money, and see something of the world. These two, Lucia Winne and Eva Bartlett, were surrounded by their friends, who had come to see them off, and as they heard the whistle of the fast-nearing train they watched anxiously for Jennie Armstrong, fearing that she would be left. But just at the last moment the old horse reached the platform and Jennie sprung out.

"I was sure you would miss the train," said

Eva, running up to her, "and that would have been too bad; we want to start with even luck. Here is the train now. I must say good-bye to them all," and she ran back to the group at the door.

Mr. Armstrong kissed his daughter after the fashion of men in parting with the dearest objects of their affections. He neither cried nor looked concerned, but, it is to be presumed that he felt quite as badly as though he had.

As the train started he stood silent and apart from the rest, a cold, misanthropic man, watching with eyes that no tear dimmed, this farewell of his only child, "sole daughter of his house and heart." He saw the three young faces at the car windows — thought how much fairer Jennie's was than the others, yet, they were pretty girls, too; and then as the cars faded away in the distance he roused himself with a sigh, wondering why any of them had ever been born.

But the three girls had no dark forebodings. They knew naught of the curse of a granted prayer!

CHAPTER II.

SWEET HOME.

"These are the hopes, that one by one
Died, even as we gave them birth!"

WHEN the cars bearing the three girls had passed quite out of sight, the group on the platform dispersed. Mr. Armstrong untied the old horse which was nibbling the scant autumn grass at halter length, and soon the three dilapidated structures — man, horse, and vehicle — were jogging back on the way home. They were nearly there when suddenly a man stepped out from a farm-gate by the roadside, and approached Mr. Armstrong with a decided gesture, commanding him to stop, which he did, waiting without a change of countenance for what was coming.

The man who approached was young, of slender, wiry frame, and with a pale, intelligent face, denoting a superabundance of nervous force. His black hair was in strange contrast to his pale blue eyes that glowed with anger or passion of some kind. His lips were thin and compressed. He placed one foot on the wheel hub, and grasped the old box seat with white, slender fingers that looked very unlike a farmer lad's.

"So Jennie's gone, has she?" he began, looking hard at Mr. Armstrong, "and not so much as said good-bye to me. I didn't expect or deserve such treatment as that, Mr. Armstrong. Were you afraid to let me know she was going off yonder? There's some difference between being an honest man's wife, and receiving the love and care of a whole lifetime, and being a stranger in that place of temptation and sin. Maybe she will find it out, too."

"I am sorry," answered Mr. Armstrong, in his cold, passionless voice; "but Jennie doesn't know her own mind. It isn't my fault that she will not be your wife, Reuben. She does not care for you, nor any one else in that way."

"She did care for me, you know she did, before that fine scamp from the city came up here to break his neck — how I wish he had ! — and have her wait on him. She always loved me, and has told me so a thousand times. You know it, Mr. Armstrong, and you were quite willing she should marry me before that fellow came! And now she's gone where she'll find him, and she'll be lost to you and to me ——"

"Stop!" said Mr. Armstrong, sternly; "Jennie is a child! She is too young to marry any man, or know what love means. She has gone to Chicago to earn her living honestly. I'm in debt over head and ears. There ain't enough picking for one on that old worn-out farm. A young girl wants a heap of things that you and I know nothing about, and when Mrs. Monroe wrote and offered Jennie this situation in her family, it seemed the best thing for her. We are as poor as poverty; there ain't no discounting that, and if anything happened to me, they couldn't earn their salt here. I can't argue with you any further, Harlow, but that's the truth of the matter. If Jennie's disappointed you, I'm sorry; but she has never told me anything. She's only just stopped playing with dolls, and would make a poor show at housekeeping, I'm thinking."

The young man drew back as the horse moved

on in obedience to a touch from the whip. "And I loved her so," he muttered, "and that infernal rascal has succeeded in getting her away. What a drivelling old dolt her father is, not to see through him!"

He turned away with a white face and clenched hands, a desperate man, all for the sake of one baby-faced girl, who, at that moment, had forgotten his existence.

Mr. Armstrong went home and put out the old horse. As he ran the wagon into its shed he saw the little book lying in the bottom. He picked it up and opened it at the fly-leaf. There was a tender inscription by the mother's hand, written only yesterday. He could not bear to tell her that Jennie had forgotten it. "I reckon she did n't want it," he said. And after all, what wonder! How can the bounding heart of youth take hold on the precious words of St. John? Later, what tender balm they are to the weary, wounded heart.

"Did she go off cheerful like?" asked Mrs. Armstrong, as her husband entered the kitchen. Her voice was shaky and her eyes suspiciously red.

"Cheerful enough," answered the man. "I guess she won't be sorry of the change. Its mighty nice riding around the country, making wreaths of autumn leaves, and drawing trees and rocks on white paper ; but grubbing among the same for a living, and not getting it, is a different thing. I'm sick enough of it for my part."

His wife did not answer him. He had been an unsuccessful lawyer, an unsuccessful politician, and a still more unsuccessful farmer. It was the man, not the luck that was wrong. He had lost friends, reputation, and money ; but his wife was his for richer or poorer, for better or worse.

"I saw Harlow," he said presently, "and he seemed cross and disappointed about Jennie. She never told him when she was going, or said good-bye. Seems to me she did n't do just right. Reuben has done a good deal for her."

"He is too tyrannical and stormy," said his wife. "The very way in which he loves Jennie would make her unhappy. She has always loved him as a brother, but she will never care for him in any other way."

"You do n't think Jennie cared for that Ross

2

Farnham, do you?" asked Mr. Armstrong, slowly, with his eyes fixed on the ceiling, as if he were reciting a lesson.

"I have not thought much about it, Richard. He paid her a great deal of attention when he got well, but there was no love-making. I know that it is through his influence Mrs. Monroe has sent for Jennie. What a splendid thing it would be if it should turn out in that way."

"Well, I do n't know. Twenty years ago, Mary, your father would have set his dog on Farnham's father if he had presumed to cross the door-sill. The son is a gentleman and not a charlatan, but I reckon he 's got some of his father's tastes. Still, money and education do a vast deal for one in this world, and he 's young. Farnham 's worth a million and we are not worth a cent. But you see, Ross Farnham can choose from among the young ladies of his own society. What chance would our little girl have against them ?"

" Such things have happened before," replied the mother. "Jennie has beauty — there 's no harm in saying that — and she is well educated. She would pick up accomplishments easily, and she is the lovingest little thing in the world," concluded this loyal heart.

"Well! I don't see exactly with your eyes, Mary;" answered her husband. "I am afraid that when Jennie sees the city ladies in their fine feathers, it will make her look very poor and dowdy."

Poor and dowdy! the mother felt as if it were blasphemy to speak in this way of her absent darling. At the same time the words brought with them a comforting assurance that in the great Garden City her little wild flower might be overlooked by evil eyes. Better be a daisy than a rose, when the king-bee comes to woo.

The old couple—old through disappointment and care and hard labor, rather than through years—sat down to supper alone for the first time. The table ware was of the poorest and plainest, and so was the fare. If there was no out-spoken sentiment of love between the two, there was respect and harmony, which are often more enduring. They had been lovers, but poverty and sorrow had come between the two so often with their spectral faces, they had frightened love away—at least, the love that expresses itself in endearment and sentiment.

"She must be nearly there by this time," said the mother, looking up at the clock.

"I reckon she is if there hasn't been any accident to the train," responded Mr. Armstrong.

Accident to the train! The mother's heart stood still a moment, then a silent prayer went up to God for her darling's protection. Strange! that she should pray. She had asked and not received all her lifetime; had wrestled for her treasures as fervently as ever Jacob did, and they had vanished from her grasp while she sought to keep them. Why should she pray? Does the Infinite God ever change any of His plans because His creatures beseech Him in anguish, on their knees? And if her darling should be brought back to her white and still, the young life expelled in a moment from its transient home to return to Him who gave it, would it not be something to thank Him for? Could not selfish love say, "She has escaped all I have suffered. She has gone without sin or sorrow to wear her crown!" Ah, dear Lord! we are human! It was the man after God's own heart who beat his breast and cried, "Would God I had died for thee."

CHAPTER III.

CHICAGO.

"Man made the town."

IT was only a six hours' ride, but many a long journey has been less important. The three girls were delighted with everybody and everything they saw. It was like going into a new world, to leave their quiet country homes, and see so many new faces and new sights. Lucia was the sober one of the trio, and kept the others within check, without at all dampening their pleasure, which was almost riotous.

It seemed to Jennie that they never would get through the streets and past the houses, all jumbled together, and into the depot, where they were greeted by a noisy gang of hackmen who stood in a row at the head of the stairs, for all the world

like a lot of school-boys in a class, each one de-
claiming his piece at the top of his voice.

"What will become of us if your brother is n't
here, Lucia," said Eva, half ready to cry, "three
lone, lorn, unprotected females. Do let us pull
our veils over our faces and make believe we are
vinegar-faced and ancient."

"Let me assume my Boston manner," said
Lucia. "Now where are my reading glasses.
There ! I am equal to a whole community of hack-
men. Now, young ladies, follow me."

But the persistent hackmen closed around the
girls, and continued to bawl out their noisy litera-
ture of travel into their stunned ears, until it
seemed to Jennie as if she had never in her life
been so frightened and bewildered. A thousand
men seemed to be pointing their whips at her,
and shouting "Right this way for the Tremont
House — Grand Pc-fic 'tel, this way, Miss; take
yer to any place yer wants to go. This way for
the Sherman 'Ouse. Get out Bill, these ladies
belong to me. 'Mercial Hotel carriage right here.
Palmer House, did you say, Miss ?" By this
time the crowd had thinned out to about a dozen,
but they impudently blocked the way, and Lucia

was ordering them, in her most authoritative schoolma'm manner to allow them to pass, when Jennie cried out "There's your brother Albert, Lucia!" A young man at once stepped forward, and the girls joined in a chorus of delight. He kissed Lucia, and shook hands heartily with the other two girls.

"Oh, Albert, those horrid men! Do send them away," cried Lucia. But they all disappeared like magic when they saw the gentleman.

"I could not imagine what they were shouting at," said Mr. Winne, laughing; "they completely hid you from view. I expect they were looking for a rich harvest from you little country girls."

"You ought to have seen Lucia, Mr. Winne," said Jennie, "I think she was going to read her diploma to them. I never saw anything so funny in my life."

"Well, Miss Jennie, you may prepare for a succession of wonderful surprises from now henceforth. Everything here is on a magnificent scale. We take the most exaggerated views of all things. But come into the reception room while I look after your baggage. You will all go home with me."

"*A thousand men seemed to be pointing their whips at her.*"—Page 23.

"Mrs. Monroe promised to meet me," said Jennie, "but there was so much confusion I expect she missed me. Of course I should not know her."

"Well, I will see that you get there safely tomorrow," said Mr. Winne. "Here is the ladies' room. Sit here for a few moments, while I look up your checks."

The place was dreary and uninviting, and a few weary looking people were waiting in the listless manner that travelers wear. The three girls sat down together, frightened and wondering. Every moment the door opened and some one came in, stared at them, at the closed ticket office, and went out. A young man in a nobby suit of gray, with a blue tie and a paper collar, leered at them like some grotesque monster, and passed harmlessly out again. Then a rather tall, well-dressed, fashionable-looking man came in, with an elegant nonchalant air, and an easy, graceful walk. He half raised his hat, in the most respectful manner, as he passed the girls, and bowed slightly, as if deprecating the intrusion. Jennie started up, clasped her hands, and then sank back into her seat. She knew this elegant gentleman, and her

heart gave a great bound.   It was Ross Farnham,
and he was looking for her.

Eva whispered to her, " It's the gentleman that
was at your house last summer.   Why do n't you
speak to him?"

Speak to him! She wished herself miles away.
Oh! how poor and insignificant she felt.   She
drew her coarse shawl about her — the shawl her
mother had robbed herself of to give to her child;
she had thought it so bright and pretty then;
now she hated it.   She tried to hide the little
hands in their cotton gloves under it.   Where,
now, was her independence of character; the jaunty
insolence, the flash and sparkle of her coquettish
beauty? She was glad Ross did not know her, and
passed her by, and yet there was a strange tremor
about her heart.   That he should not recognize
her was humiliating, too.   Then, while she was
shrinking back between her companions, he turned
and saw her, and came quickly toward her, holding out his well-gloved hands with a pleasant
effusion of manner.

" Miss Armstrong! I did not expect to see you
with company.   I am very glad to welcome you
to Chicago.   I understood Mrs. Monroe to say

you were alone. She sent me down for you, but indeed I am very glad to see you again and to be of service. I have the carriage here, waiting."

All this time he was shaking hands with that warm, cordial, yet respectful manner peculiar to him. Jennie returned his greeting timidly, without a shade of the audacious coquetry with which she tormented her rustic admirers. Then she introduced him to her friends, and he proved to be acquainted with Lucia's brother, Mr. Winne, who greeted him very coolly, however, when he came, and seemed disposed to insist on retaining Jennie under his protection, at least until the next morning. Ross Farnham would not listen to this, and Jennie made her adieus, promising to see her friends often; and the carriage rolled away with her seated by the side of Mr. Farnham.

It was all like Heaven to poor Jennie! The easy luxurious motion of the comfortable equipage, the liveried driver, the gay panorama of city streets all alight, seen now for the first time, the handsome impassioned face opposite, and the pleasant dark eyes that she felt were regarding her with kindly interest! the girl forgot that she was poor and dowdy; that she had come to Chicago to be a sort of upper servant; and, leaning back on the brown satin cushions, she took it all in as an enchanted dream. Then the carriage stopped, and Mr. Farnham assisted her out, and they entered a great handsome hall, with plate glass windows filled with a glittering show of frosted silver, glass, and fruit. There was a long *salon*, where gentlemen were seated at small tables, eating and reading. They passed through the entire length of this to the further end, where ladies and gentlemen were seated together at the tables. Ross Farnham installed Jennie comfortably before one of the marble stands, and bade the attentive colored waiter furnish the best supper the place afforded. Jennie was half frightened, and wholly awed by the splendor about her; by the great glistening chandeliers, all alight with prismatic hues; by the lofty frescoed ceilings, and imposing array of tables, glittering with silver and cut glass; and by the colored attendants running noiselessly about. Somehow the child grew dazzled and frightened by it all. Ross Farnham saw the look of perplexity on the girl's face, and said gently:

" I knew you must be hungry, and so brought
you here for supper, as it is not at all likely Mrs.
Monroe would think to offer you any. And now
you must promise to eat," he added, as the waiter
appeared with a heavily laden tray. " Here is
some tea, strong and hot, and a pot of chocolate,
and fried oysters. Do you like them? And French
rolls and broiled quail; " and he helped her
daintily.

" Then this is not Mrs. Monroe's?" asked Jennie,
sipping her chocolate and looking about with very
wide open eyes.

Ross Farnham was delighted with the girl's
naivette. "Not exactly," he said, laughing.
" Her *salle-a-mangé* is hardly so spacious. This
is Thompson's. All the good people come here
to eat. There is an odor of sanctity in the very
walls."

" There is an odor of cooking, too," laughed Jennie, who was growing very much at her ease. " I
know one thing I shall miss here, and that is the
fresh air; it is exactly six hours since I have had
a mouthful of it."

" Indeed you will not," answered Ross. " I
will take you out to ride where the air is just as

pure and good as at Newton.   I have a bay trot-
ter that I have reserved for this."

Jennie smiled with a look of intense satisfac-
tion.   She had heard dreadful stories of city life,
of young girls enticed away from their country
homes, and never heard of again.   Of elegant
and handsome men who went about in the guise
of angels of light, but were fiends of darkness.
Of traps set for unwary souls — gilded traps, into
which they sometimes walked most willingly.
She had been so well drilled into terror of all
these nameless ills that she felt strong and elate
sitting there with her friend, Ross Farnham, to
protect her, and all this atmosphere of luxury and
respectability about her.   She grew chatty and
confidential; recalled little incidents of the past
summer, when they went harvesting and nutting
together, and asked innumerable questions about
Mrs. Monroe and her surroundings, and laughed
her own cheery laugh.

Ross Farnham was charmed !   The child did
not know her own value; did not know that she
was as lovely as an angel.   But she did know, by
a girl's quick intuition, that she was acceptable
to Ross Farnham; that he did not think her poor

or countryfied or shabby. He, the elegant man of the world, had spent many an hour willingly in her society, nor had he ever given her a word or a look that was not respectful, while there was ever an undertone of tenderness that set her heart beating wildly. There was that same manner now, as he clasped her coarse shawl about her as though it were the mantle of a princess, and handed her, the little country rustic ! back into the throne-like carriage waiting at the door in the strong gas-light. As she turned to look out a moment into the lighted streets she saw a woman, young, fair, dressed as if for a ball, in silk and lace and glittering jewels. She came out from the shadow and stood a moment gazing at the carriage as it rolled away, and there was such a look of misery and hate on her haggard face, such a revelation of a soul in the throes of moral death, that Jennie turned shuddering away and nestled closer to Ross Farnham for protection.

In a short time the carriage stopped, and now at a handsome residence on the West Side.

" This is Mrs. Monroe's," said Mr. Farnham, as he assisted Jennie from the carriage and accompanied her up the steps. He rang the bell, and a servant opened the door. She was expecting them, and at once relieved Jennie of her satchel.

"Are you coming in, Mr. Farnham?" she asked respectfully.

"Not to night, Esther; I will see Mrs. Monroe to-morrow. I suppose she is as well as usual."

" *She came out from the shadow and stood a moment looking
at the carriage as it rolled away.*" — Page 31.

CHAPTER IV.

HUNTING A SITUATION.

EVA BARTLETT spent two or three days at Mrs. Winne's with Lucia, and then turned her steps toward the situation she desired to find. She had hoped that Lucia's brother would help her in this, and that perhaps Lucia herself would be able to go out with her in her quest at the various stores, but she soon learned that Chicago people are a very busy people, and that for every situation vacant, there at least two hundred applicants, and that as a rule the merchants care much less about the necessities and sensibilities of their clerks than they do about their capacities as good saleswomen. Mr. Winne filled a government position, being an employee of the post-office. He did find time to see the superintendent of schools and introduce his sister Lucia to him, and he gave Eva a slip of paper containing the names of the

leading dry-goods houses, with the street and
number attached, telling her as he did so that she
was welcome to stay at his house until she found
a situation. His wife, however, was a peevish
invalid with her arms full of little children —
luxúries his small salary did not justify — and
she spent the most of her time in berating their
one servant, and cheapening the prices of living,
with the results of which she regaled her husband when he went home at night tired and
embarrassed. Both girls hated the stifled, sordid
atmosphere, and determined to get out of it as
soon as possible.

Lucia went first. As she passed a good exam-
ination and obtained a first-class certificate, she
was at once called upon as a substitute for a
teacher who was ill, and her services giving sat-
isfaction she retained the place, the convalescent
teacher being placed in a department where the
work was lighter. Lucia found it convenient
to pay the same board which her brother's wife
demanded of her, at a place nearer to the school,
and in a family whose joys and sorrows were not
a matter of traffic. In her own little room she
could rest and enjoy herself after her own fash-

ion, and she soon found that a teacher is always welcome in the best society. Education does that, at least, for its servitors.

"Do you want anybody in the store?" This was the form of Eva's address as she walked from one place to another, following the direction on her slip of paper. Of course, the answer was no, and sometimes it was accompanied by a contemptuous shrug of the shoulders. At last she entered a large dry-goods store on the west side of State street, and asked the same question of a lady who stood behind a show case. "You will have to see the proprietor," answered the young woman, gently. "He is there talking to a salesman," pointing in the direction. "Wait till he turns away, and then speak to him."

"Oh! do you think he will want me?" asked Eva, almost hysterically. She was *so* tired of tramping the streets, and getting no encouragement. The young lady behind the show case looked at her attentively. Eva was rather tall and large, a blonde with violet eyes and a profusion of wavy hair, too fair for golden but very soft and pretty in its effect. She was a girl who could dress up attractively in a very little, but

would look magnificent in rich and elegant cos-
tumes. The pale young lady whom Eva had
addressed scanned her with professional eyes,
and at her eager " oh, do you think he will want
me ?" answered sorrowfully, " I think he will."
Something in the answer restrained Eva's glad-
ness.

" Is the place so very hard ?" she asked.

" Hard enough," replied the other, dusting
out her show case, and then she turned away to
wait on a lady who dragged any amount of pea-
cock finery after her. By this time the proprietor of the store had finished his instructions to
his salesman. This was Eva's chance. With her
heart in her mouth she approached the gentleman and asked the usual question.

He was a handsome, elderly man, stout and
florid, with a profusion of curly, iron-gray hair.
He wore a pair of handsome, gold-rimmed
glasses, and he looked at her a full minute
before speaking, then he answered her question
by asking another.

" What can you do ?"

For answer Eva gave him her letters of reference from the country storekeeper who had

employed her. He stood a moment in deep thought.

"I hardly know. It seems as though I had heard them say they needed a good figure in the shawl room. You would do," he said, turning Eva round as if she were indeed a lay figure. "Come with me," he added, and went directly to the young lady to whom Eva had first spoken. "Miss Holmes, if there is a vacancy in the shawl department, will you try this young woman? You can instruct her in the usual duties, and let her know the rules. I will see you to-morrow," and he bowed courteously and withdrew.

Had the skies fallen? Was this weary, disconsolate Eva Bartlett, who had trudged away a week, after what seemed a forlorn hope, now an employee of the flourishing dry-goods house of Bates & Rockwell? The sad, stern face behind the counter recalled her.

"Where are you stopping?" asked Miss Holmes, putting her laces in order while she talked. Eva informed her, and also told of her necessity of at once finding a boarding place. "You can board where I do, at the Woman's Home, on Jackson street."

"Is it a hospital?" asked Eva, the name suggesting some public institution.

Miss Holmes smiled a little at this. "It is, after a sort," she said, "a hospital for the halt and the blind. At least, it is a refuge from the average boarding-house keeper. You can have a comfortable half-room for four dollars a week, and if you like music, a piano to practice on. There are no men in the establishment, except a caterer, and the women all hate each other cordially; but you need have nothing to do with any of them unless you wish. You can come to-night if you please."

Eva thanked the young lady and promised to be there. Then she went back to Mr. Winne's and reported progress. Her friends here considered her particularly fortunate. After tea she packed up her small wardrobe and made her adieux. Unlike Lucia, she felt sorry to go. She was accustomed to children, and liked the sticky caresses of these little ones, and she felt sure she should prefer the disordered atmosphere of the family to the restricted air of the Home. Yet she felt that it was best for her to go.

Mr. Winne accompanied her to her new residence, and saw her safe in Miss Holmes' keeping. Then he left her with a kind invitation to spend her Sundays and holidays with 'Lucia at his house.

Eva thought the Home a palace. The great, warm parlors, the halls well lighted, and furnished so luxuriously, seemed to her the embodiment of all comfort. Some of the boarders were entertaining company in the parlors ; some were trilling at the pianos ; others walked arm in arm through the halls. All looked comfortable and happy and seemed to consider it a home indeed.

"I have made an exchange, and you are to share my room," said Miss Holmes, as she led the way there. " It is small, as you see," throwing open the door, " but we can manage. It is large enough and fine enough for shop girls, as you will soon find."

She spoke bitterly, and her manner impressed Eva disagreeably. She needed to be re-assured and comforted this first night among strangers, but she felt as though constantly menaced by some hidden danger.

But she was a brave girl, and not accustomed to thinking merely of her own comfort, so she unpacked her trunk and hung up her few dresses in her half of the closet. Miss Holmes watched her but did not offer to assist. She seemed tired out, and lay on the small lounge as utterly prostrate as if she never expected to rise again. Still, she noted each garment as it appeared and commented on it. There were only three. The last was a black alpaca, plainly but neatly made.

"That will do for the store," said Miss Holmes. "We all wear black. It does not show wear nor dust, and then with different sets of collars and cuffs, you can always appear to advantage. Now let me advise you how to dress for the first week, after that you will see for yourself. Wear that black dress with blue ribbons, and do your hair up in a coil with a black velvet band around the front. That light hair of yours will dress splendidly. Oh! child! what did your mother send you here for? Do you know that you have walked right into the lion's den, poor little lamb?"

Eva's large, intelligent eyes filled with tears. "Is it such a wicked place?" she said. "Well! I am not afraid. I mean to attend to my work all day, and at night I shall be here with you,

and you will help me to be good — I am sure
you will ;" and she knelt affectionately by the
low couch and patted the hand that hung white
and limp over the side,

But the hand was instantly withdrawn, and
Margaret Holmes rose stiffly to a sitting posture
and a bright red spot burned fiercely in either
cheek.

"You do not know what you are talking
about," she said, coldly. Then she suddenly
changed her mood and sobbed aloud, and Eva
heard her saying, "Let this be my compensation," as she clasped the surprised girl to
her heart for a moment. "And now you must
go to bed and to sleep, for to-morrow will come
early. Yes, dear. child ! I will help you to be
good."

CHAPTER V.

A WOMAN WITH A MISSION !

JENNIE followed the servant up stairs to Mrs. Monroe's room. She expected to find a delicate invalid, supported by pillows; but, much to her surprise, she saw a large, fair woman, quite elaborately dressed, and looking in a high state of health and preservation. The lady came forward with much *empressement* to meet Jennie, took both her hands, drew the girl to her, and, looking intently at her, said, in a low, sweet voice:

"So this is my little waiting maid. Do you think you will be happy here with me, Jennie? You see I know your name. My cousin, Ross Farnham, has told me about you, and I have had a long letter from your mother. Mr. Farnham is always talking about the little girl that took such good care of him when his horse threw him. Were n't you dreadfully frightened?"

Poor Jennie had stood appalled during this voluble harangue, held at arm's length by the fair, large woman, who was regarding her all the time with critical attention. In reply to her question she said:

"We did think he was killed at first," and a shudder passed over her, "but when the doctor came, he said he was only stunned. It was mother who took care of him. I only walked out with him and read to him."

"Well, I am glad to have you here. I like the society of young girls. Do you know you are to wait on me, bring up my breakfast, take care of these rooms, and read the papers aloud, and help me with my correspondence? I am nearly worked to death now. I am Secretary of the Women's League, President of the B. W. A. S., and Visitor at the Orphans' Home. You must read my lecture on the Progressive Spirit of the Age. I shall make a business woman of you, Jennie. You are only a pretty doll now. That is what all women are until they are emancipated. Now what can you do?"

' At first Jennie felt inclined to say, Nothing! her small stock of accomplishments seemed so poor by contrast. Then she remembered that she had come here to work and earn money, and she informed Mrs. Monroe that she could write, and sew neatly, and do light branches of house-work. She could read well, for her father had instructed her, and play the melodeon for Sunday-School airs, and draw a little, and group autumn leaves and ferns prettily. That was all.

"Why you are quite a wonder, Jennie," said the lady, condescendingly. "I will teach you to be self-reliant, and make use of the talents given to you. Do you think you will like to live here?"

Jennie looked about the room a moment before answering. It was gorgeous with the glitter of cut glass and ornaments. Mirrors in every available place; brackets at every angle, with lovely little statuettes on them; flowers in bright bloom; books in handsome bindings; a large, lace-draped bed, with flying cupids hovering near, hung by invisible wires; and the large, handsome mistress of it all looking at her earnestly She felt that she had entered upon a sphere of life that was completely and enthrall-ingly new; but whether she should like it, or not, how could she tell?

"I hope I shall," she answered at last, having recalled the gift of speech, " and I will try to do exactly as you want me to. Mother said you would have patience with me, for I should be new and awkward at first."

"You could not be awkward if you tried," said Mrs. Monroe kindly. She had a morbid desire for a *protégé*. This beautiful untrained girl would bring additional *éclat* to her charita-ble career.

Jennie felt a little homesick pang as she spoke of her mother, and the dew that rises so often from the heart suffused her eyes. But Mrs. Monroe drew her toward another room and opened the door into a perfect little bower of a chamber.

"This is your room, Jennie," she said, "I like to have you near me, in case of a sudden illness. You see it opens from mine. Mr. Monroe is away so much that I like to have some one within call."

"It is just lovely," murmured Jennie in a

pleased tone, looking with rapture on the bright
carpet, a pattern with violets on a drab ground,
on the large white curtains, the pretty toilet
table and the knick-knacks upon it.

"I am glad you like it. You can hang your
things in the closet; and, as it is late, and you
must be tired, good night;" and Mrs. Monroe
shut the door between them as she spoke.

"She never asked me to sit down," thought
Jennie; "I wonder if that is city manners.
Never mind! This is more than I ever dreamed
of in my life, before."

She inspected everything with a girl's careful
notice, and then, being really tired from the
excitement and novelty, undressed, and was soon
ready to sleep in the pretty white bed. But first
she knelt down and asked God to take care of
her. She had never omitted this habit since her
mother had first joined her hands at her knee.
Perhaps it was only a habit.. Perhaps she had
hard work to feel that she was a sinner, and fix
her mind upon God as a frowning Judge. I
think myself she asked Him to take care of her
in the tone of a spoiled child, that did not believe in any danger. All the same, she did not

forget to kneel under the strange roof, and with a pleasant sleepiness taking possession of her, to add her little prayer to the countless petitions going up to the unchanged and unchangable God.

Will He take care of her?

It was not of Him she thought as her head sunk into the soft pillow, or of His infinite splendor. Her poor little worldly heart was filled with the glory of one of His creatures. One fond thought for the dear mother at home, and the rest for Ross Farnham.

The next morning Jennie was awake and up early to attend to her duties. Mrs. Monroe, seen by daylight, was a disappointment — a physical wreck. She had grown old in the service of society, and her face was wrinkled and pallid in the morning light. Its expression, too, was uncertain and discontented. A *blasé* woman is infinitely more an object of pity than a *blasé* man. Paint and powder lend a temporary enchantment to the features, but they kill the soul. Jennie's first lesson in the art of enamelling and making up was a novel experience. It was her first initiation into the impurity of fashion, and she could not quite disguise her contempt for this modern Jezebel. She wrote a piquant description home to her mother, who answered that her own grandmother, who was a good woman, had worn powder and patches!

"*She had been patted by Jew and Gentile until it seemed sometimes as if she must drop.*"—Page 49.

CHAPTER VI.

"ONLY A SHOP GIRL."

EVA had been installed in the cloak-room for several weeks. She had tried on every garment in the shape of cloak or shawl, and had stood like a wooden block, while impatient fingers pulled her this way and that. She had been patted by Jew and Gentile until it seemed sometimes as if she must drop, from sheer weariness, an inert mass at their feet. The woman who wanted a cloak could sit comfortably while she looked at the fit of it on Eva's shapely form, but she must stand, stand from morning till night, until her back ached, and her limbs were weary, and her feet were swollen to nearly twice their natural size. She could not eat her supper when she went home at night until she had plunged those poor, aching feet into a tub of cold water, and bound a towel, dipped in the same

4 (49)

cooling fluid about her throbbing temples. Margaret Holmes forgot her own weariness and trouble in helping Eva. Her feet were hardened by their long years of waiting. So she thought was her heart. But there was one tender spot left, and Eva had reached it, happily for herself.

It was a hard place. Eva found that out soon enough. It is said that the sick inmates of a hospital loathe each other. They have no sympathy for their duplicate misery. So those who are compelled to work side by side in a store all day, serving as puppets, poorly paid puppets at that, learn to look with contempt on each other. Eva found herself in an atmosphere of open or suppressed discontent. Her own endeavors to be pleasant and courteous in her intercourse with others were met with open criticism or sneering suspicion; so she determined to give her exclusive attention to her work, and at least merit the approbation of her employers; and she soon learned to be always smiling and agreeable to all probable or possible customers. She worked steadily from eight in the morning until six at night, with an hour for lunch. She was not expected, nor, indeed, allowed to sit down during the whole time, except at the hour of noon. When not engaged in selling a cloak, or having one fitted upon her, she had the boxes to keep in order, the counters and tables and changes of buttons and trimmings to look after, or the head of the department to wait upon. For this service she received seven dollars a week, with an ultimate promise of ten, if the season was good, and she was found to be worth it. In the next department another saleswoman, a quiet, sad-faced girl of eighteen, received twelve; but she belonged to a family who had formerly been in fashionable society, and could influence a large amount of trade among the fashionable people, some of whom cut her to the heart by their condescending patronage; while others, and they were among the really best, put themselves out to do her a favor, and never let her know it. She could speak three languages, and was an accomplished musician. Eva liked her quiet, lady-like manner, and the two girls tacitly agreed never to make it any harder for each other; but, beyond the courtesy of business, they made no further acquaintance. The fact was, the dependant, who had seen better days, had nothing to look forward to, and was dying of hopelessness, while Eva had everything in the future — a home and independence for herself and her widowed mother. Seven dollars a week to the girl who had never before earned but two, was a beginning that promised well.

Mr. Bates, the senior partner, had taken considerable notice of Eva. He had himself explained her duties, and on several occasions had watched her making sales, and suggested certain methods. Eva listened respectfully, but when he came near, and she looked up into his face, there seemed some oppression in the air. There was a look of intense admiration in his dark, half-veiled eyes; a cruel friendliness in the tender regard of his look. It seemed as if Margaret Holmes knew by intuition when he was near Eva, for then she had always some excuse to draw near, and Mr. Bates would compress his handsome lips, give his stately shoulders a half-contemptuous shrug, and saunter away. No girl in that store would have dared him as Miss Holmes did, and none hated him with as just a cause.

At the Home Eva found a comfortable enough

resting-place. She liked the management, but she did not enjoy the aggregation of poverty. At night the little tables were filled with a tired community of toilers; young girls, old maids, widows, wives who had no husbands, and colorless neutral women, who seemed never to have had a childhood, but were perpetual dwellers in the arid region of middle age. Never a man among them, nor a little child. Heavens! what a life! Of their heart-burnings and histories, Eva knew nothing. They were nearly all dully uninteresting to her. Even to themselves life was either a battle or a blank! Some few were young girls, like Eva, who expected little, but deserved much. After tea Eva and Miss Holmes would, perhaps, sit a few moments in the parlors and listen to some music; but generally they went at once to their little box of a room and sat there all the evening, walled in, hearing gay voices, but not joining in any mirth themselves. Eva longed to see the inside of a theatre; but Margaret Holmes had objected to the one invitation she had received from the spruce young cashier.

"It is the way all girls begin," she had said. "I cannot bear that you should follow their example;" and Eva had denied herself the coveted pleasure, rather than appear ungrateful.

But it did seem at times that life ought to hold something better and brighter than this monotonous work-a-day existence. Eva longed, with downright homesickness, for a romp with the boys and girls at home, a breezy run to the village post office, a downright good time, in spite of hard work, and there was always a tempter ready to show her the kaleidoscope of pleasure. From such thoughts as these she would raise her eyes to see Margaret Holmes observing her like some grim spectre of fate, saying "Thou shalt not! Thou shalt not!"

CHAPTER VII.

IN THE TOILS.

MRS. MONROE'S room was darkened, that lady being prostrate with a severe headache. Jennie was writing by a faint gas jet, directing a great pile of business envelopes, in a fair, round hand. She has changed somewhat since we saw her last. Her too vivid country color has toned down to a mere tinting of the oval cheek. She looks more womanly, is far more beautiful than formerly, but it is plainly visible that this mode of life does not suit her. She is looking careworn and tired. Her work, to tell the truth, is horribly distasteful to her. She hates the very name of reformers and reform. The makeshifts of this house are pitiable, and the charities of its mistress wear a mantle to conceal it from the world. Jennie had tried her best to become interested in foundling babies and old ladies' homes, and had really gone upon missionary investigations in the spirit of a true reformer; but she could not find any pleasure or comfort in the final emancipation of her sex through the arena of political glory. To be the wife of the man she loved, and the mother of his children, seemed to her an infinitely higher station for any woman, than a position as judge of a supreme court, editor of a newspaper, or founder of all the Good Samaritan societies in the world. Mrs. Monroe called her an idiot, and gave up proselyting her. Jennie did her work well. There could be no fault found with that; but it was impossible to please the captious woman whose life chords were all dissonant; so the young girl bore with her as best she might — served her conscientiously for the pay that was slow in coming, and tried her best to regulate the ill-assorted household, while Mrs. Monroe read, and dreamed, and theorized her life away.

As she now sits and writes in the half-darkened room, some one is looking at her through the half opened door. She is writing busily, her rosy lips compressed, her lovely head set coquet-

tishly on one side, in the exact pose that paint-
ers seek. Her rosy fingers are blurred with ink,
only making her more deliciously lovely.

So thinks Ross Farnham, as he stands there
watching her, himself unseen. There is a
Psyche on the wall-bracket just above her head,
but it suffers in comparison with her. An
exquisite ideal painting of summer, rose-crowned
and warm-tinted, with lovely luminous eyes,
and baby dimples, looked something like her;
but when did a painted picture blush and smile
as this other did, lifting her eyes and seeing
him there?

"You must not come." She put one small
inky finger on her pouting lips and went to
meet him. "Mrs. Monroe has such a headache,
and I have been as still as a mouse all the afternoon."

He imprisoned both hands — it had come to
to this, then — and looked at her with greedy
admiration.

"And you shall not sit here another minute,
such a day as it is for a ride; cool and crisp,
with a tang in the air like wine. Run and get

your things on. I want you to go out on the Boulevard."

"But Mrs. Monroe will need me. I have not finished my work yet," said Jennie, looking up into the handsome, dangerous face, and seeing as in a vision, a long stretch of smooth road, and two very happy people bowling along it.

Ross Farnham's face flushed angrily. He was not accustomed to beg for favors of this kind. He flung open the door, and said:

"Maria, I want Jennie for an hour on the Boulevard," coolly ignoring possible denial.

Mrs. Monroe was indignant at her sudden awakening, and at Jennie for permitting it; but she had no power to restrain her cousin's wishes, so she gave an ungracious permission for Jennie to get ready.

When Jennie had gone, Mrs. Monroe sat up, gathered her handsome negligé robe about her, and looked angrily at her cousin. He, in return, surveyed her critically, and coolly remarked:

"You are looking exceedingly well for an invalid, Maria."

"Thank you! I don't imagine you came here solely to compliment my appearance, Ross, and even if you did, I wish you would stay away. You will spoil that girl with your attentions, whether you mean anything or nothing. I really believe she is indulging in hopes ridiculously above her position, even now."

"I am doing a simple act of kindness, as you well know. When I was in her neighborhood, a miserable, peevish, sick man, she did everything in her power to make time pass pleasantly for me."

"And you repaid the family in coin such people love best. You helped her impecunious old father, and you gave me no peace until I sent for the daughter. Ross Farnham, let this girl alone. I will send her back to her poverty, rather than see her harmed by you."

For all answer, he got up, crossed the room, and stood before his cousin, as she sat thrown back in a lounging chair. "Shall I tell her," he asked in a low voice, "the story of Anna Lester?"

"No! no!" cried his cousin, excitedly, clasping her hands in supplication. "In mercy, no!"

"Then leave Jennie to me," he retorted sternly. "I think," he sneered, "that you church goers

consider some souls pre-ordained to be saved,
and some to be lost.   You may consider her one
of the elect, or —— "

He did not finish the sentence.   Jennie, radiant and blushing, came into the room.   She
busied herself about Mrs. Monroe for a moment,
bending down her blushing face to whisper " I
will not be long away," and leaving a small,
pure kiss on that lady's artistically powdered
cheek.

Of what strange material are women made.
At that moment, when the young and tender
heart of the girl went out in gratitude to the
older woman for being even the remote cause of
her happiness, the older one was coming very
near to envying and hating her, because the girl
was just entering upon a threshold which she
had crossed.

As Ross Farnham helped Jennie into the comfortable open carriage, he smiled to himself.
The little brown straw hat, with its pigeon
wing, plucked and pressed by herself ; the short,
coarse jacket, made of her mother's old cloak ;
the cheap, washed pin that clasped a too bright
ribbon, grated on the man's nice appreciation of

dress, but they did not appeal to his more ob-
tuse moral sense. Miss Badger would have
worn seal skin, and the finest ostrich plume
would have trailed over her dainty shoulders,
and her long, slim fingers would have been cased
in pearl-colored kids. But who of them all had
so pretty and piquant a face, so delicately curved
a chin, so lily like a throat. And to this girl
everything was new and fresh.

CHAPTER VIII.

"This is not a fit match," quoth Robin Hood,
"That you do seem to make her."
"Oh, loving heart trust on."

HERE'S a letter for you, Mrs. Armstrong. From Jennie, I think," said Reuben Harlow, walking in upon the old couple one evening some weeks after Jennie had gone. "I just stepped into Burt's a moment, and he asked me to bring it up."

"Thank you, Reuben; sit by while we read it," and the proud mother adjusted her glasses carefully and read the four pages of closely written paper with the most careful attention, before she ventured upon any part of it aloud. It was a wonderful letter — bright, cheery, full of good news, and folded up in it was a crisp five dollar bill — Mrs. Monroe's first installment of Jennie's wages. It was sent with a gleeful little message,

and the mother kissed it and put it in her bosom
as a precious treasure.

"Now what does she say, Mary?" asked Mr.
Armstrong, becoming impatient as the mother
seemed inclined to read the letter to herself once
more. "Reuben would like to know, too."

"It's good news, Richard," answered the
mother, smiling to herself. "I can hardly
believe it yet, it is such good news. Did n't I
tell you our little girl would have good luck?
She is to be Ross Farnham's wife!"

"Ross Farnham's wife!" Mr. Armstrong
looked almost as happy as the mother. "Well,
that is news! No more poverty and hardship
for her then! I can hardly believe it. Cheer
up, Reuben! there are plenty of girls who will
be glad to welcome your attentions. Do n't
look so glum, man!"

"Does she say he is to *marry* her?" asked
Reuben, looking hard at Mrs. Armstrong.

"Why, its the same thing," answered the
mother, finding the place in the letter. Here
she says, "Ross offered me a splendid fur cloak,
mother, but I thought you would not want me
to accept anything of that sort before we were

married." And, again: "Ross has selected a diamond ring. He says it is worth many thousands of dollars. Only think! that for your little Jennie. He has just brought me such a lovely bouquet. Oh, dear mother, I am too happy! When Mrs. Monroe lectures me I do not cry as I used to, but just smile to think how different it will all be when I am Ross' wife. I have promised him not to say a word about it yet to anybody in the world; but, of course, he did not think I would keep it from you or father."

"I am sorry for you, Reuben," said Mrs. Armstrong; "but you see it was not to happen. I won't say that you might not have made her a better husband than Mr. Farnham, but he took her fancy last summer, and it seems he has chosen her above all the girls he knows. I never was one to think money makes people wicked. I believe the poor have more temptations to overcome than the rich. I think Jennie will not be spoiled by prosperity."

"She won't belong to us any more, Mary," said the father, with some latent regret in his tones. "So all this time we've been worrying

about her, she has had her bread cut and
buttered on both sides. Well! she's a good
girl ; thanks to you, Mary, and though we are
poor, we've never done anything disgraceful,
and I guess her blood is bluer than Ross Farnham's."

"Oh, Richard! It is such a comfort to me
to feel that Jennie will be taken care of, no
matter what happens to us. It has been such
a terror to my mind that she might have to
battle alone with the world."

"I thought you were a Christian, Mrs. Armstrong," said Reuben Harlow, wearily. "Of
what use are faith and prayer, if the Bible
promises are false ?"

"When Jennie was born, Reuben, I committed her to the care of God, but I never stopped
working for her myself. No human soul is
ever safe from temptation. It needs watching
and praying for all the time."

"Its my opinion Jennie needs your prayers
more than ever now," continued Reuben. "You
know I never believed in her going to the city.
It is no place for young and handsome girls,
who are poor and unprotected. I shall be glad

5

to hear of her good fortune when I know it to
be such. She is a thousand times too good for
Ross Farnham." He took his hat as he spoke,
and with an abrupt good-night left the farm-
house.

"Reuben seems a good deal cut up about
Jennie," said Mr. Armstrong, taking up his
daughter's letter, and preparing to read it carefully. "It is strange how things turn out.
Who would have thought when that awkward
bay ran off and threw Ross Farnham at our
gate, that it would ever take such a turn as
this."

The father read the letter and went to bed,
but the mother sat up till far into the night,
marking out a path of roses for her child.

Reuben Harlow went home and as usual
found his mother sitting up for him. He went
and sat down by her and said, abruptly:

"I'm going up to Chicago to-morrow, mother,
to find out the truth about Jennie Armstrong.
She has written home that she expects to be
married to Ross Farnham. I took the letter up
there myself to-night. I meant to tell them
how tongues were wagging here about her,

but I had n't the heart to. I 'm going myself
to find out the truth."

"And when you have found it out, Reuben,
what good will it do ? Is she the only woman
in the world, that you must spend your time
running after her ? What good will it do you ?
She went off and never said a good-bye to you,
and she won't know you in the city. It 's her
nature. She 's fickle minded and ungrateful, is
Jennie Armstrong, and you know it, Ruby."

"I do n't care if she is, mother. She is the
one woman in the world for me, and I will not
see her go to destruction without lifting a finger
to save her. I 'll find out whether her fine lover
intends to marry her—curse him. And I 'll
warn her of the evil things said about her.
Poor child ! she has n't the least idea what such
wickedness means. If her father had a grain
of common sense, he would have kept her at
home and taken care of her."

"What did she go to the city for ?" asked his
mother, angrily. "There 's enough to do at
home. But, no ; I s'pose the girl must have
fine dresses, and ribbons, and laces, like the rest
of them. Reputation goes for nothing. I 've

seen her droning about with that Farnham, walking, and riding, and picking flowers, while her mother cooked, and washed, and ironed at home. It shows a bad heart to my thinking."

" It was because of her inherited delicacy of constitution, and the way her mother brought her up. She could never stand drudging. Why, her hands are like a lady's," said this valiant defender of the absent girl.

" Inherited fiddlesticks !" retorted his mother. She was a good woman, but had outlived the romance of youth. "And you want to marry this baby-handed girl and bring her here over me. Reuben Harlow, you are an ungrateful son."

" No, I 'm not, mother," answered the young man, sorrowfully. " You would have no harder work to do, if I married Jennie. Oh, God ! how I wish I could. I 've loved her since she was that high," measuring the height with his hand. " Since she first said, ' I 'll be your little wife, Ruby;' and now, and now, mother, I tell you I must go and find out what she means to do, or I shall go mad. This fellow Farnham is following her up and giving her presents, and taking her out to ride. Now I am going to find out if he intends to marry her. If he does, it's all right, I'll come back and never speak her name again. But if he—if he dares to make her a thing so vile"—he started up digging his nails into the palms of his hands—"why, there'll be a short reckoning between us—that's all!"

Mrs. Harlow was frightened by this depth of passion. It seemed to her that his pale student father stood there instead of Reuben, the boy she had reared alone. She felt sorry for the love that was wasted, and indignant at the girl who had thrown him over for another. True, Jennie had not been his plighted wife, save in the extravagant play of their childhood, but he had always been her sworn friend, boy and man, and until the unlucky hour when a runaway horse threw Ross Farnham at her father's gate.

The next morning Reuben packed a crumpled leather satchel with necessary clothing. Then he went to a drawer, took out a small single ball pistol, and without a word cleaned and loaded it. He saw his mother watching him anxiously. "For thieves!" he said quietly; "the city is full of them."

CHAPTER IX.

'When shall we three meet again."

IT was Thanksgiving Day in the State of Illinois. The offices and stores in the city were all closed, and everybody that could, took a holiday. There was a grand exodus of all who had country homes or friends to visit, and the odor of roast turkey was strong in the land. It was a busy time for housewives, and a fearful epoch in poultry life; but it is pleasant to feel that one is sacrificed in a good cause.

The home of Lucia Winne's brother underwent a grand transformation for the occasion, and fairly glowed under its decoration of red berries rifled from the mountain ash, and beautifully varied autumn leaves. They were sent from the old homestead at Newton, accompanied by a generous supply of apples and the grand sultan of the turkey dominion. Said turkey was now smoking hot in the oven, crisp and brown, and pervading the atmosphere with its delicious odors.

All the little sticky children in the household had been picked up, washed and dried, set in a row and counted, and told to be good till Aunt Lucia came. They piled themselves up in the front windows, after awhile, and flattened their noses against the window-panes. Just as it was growing dark they all cried out in chorus, "There's three Aunt Lucias comed!" The three proved to be Lucia, Eva, and Jennie, who were invited to spend the evening and night in Mr. Winne's family.

There was so much noise after this that poor, peevish little Mrs. Winne would have gone distracted, only she was accustomed to earthquakes of sound. It was the first unrestrained intercourse the three girls had enjoyed since they came to the city, and they were determined to make the most of it. They talked and laughed a great deal, and kissed all the babies, and gave them candy, making them stickier than ever. As soon as Mr. Winne came in — he had been

cracking nuts in some remote corner — they all
went out to the comfortable dining-room and
sat down, without ceremony, to a real home
dinner.

"Oh!" cried Jennie, merrily, "what a beautiful turkey!"

"And what lovely cranberry jelly," responded
Eva.

"And what delicious celery," said Lucia, with
her usual propriety.

"And what silly geese!" exclaimed Mr.
Winne, flourishing his carving-knife as if it had
been a baton.

"The cackling of geese saved Rome," answered Lucia, sententiously.

"Well, it won't save Turkey," retorted the
master of the house, and in merry mood they
attacked the feast set before them. Even Mrs.
Winne caught the spirit of jollity, and forgot to
administer reproof or to grumble.

"Who do you think I saw yesterday?" asked
Eva, when they were finishing the dessert.
She looked at Jennie as she spoke.

"Any one we all know?" answered Jennie,
blushing slightly.

"Yes. It was Reuben Harlow; and he looked as if he had been ill. He was stalking along State street reading the signs. I ran after him half a block, but he walked so fast I lost sight of him. Now what do you suppose brought him to Chicago?"

"Why, you know he often comes here on business," said Jennie indifferently, but feeling, somehow, as if she were to blame.

"I saw him myself," said Mr. Winne, "and asked him to come up here to-day, but he hardly seemed to hear me; and, by the way, Jennie, he asked me several questions about you. I mean 't to tell you. I wonder what has changed Reuben so much. He used to be as lively as any of us, and was always a favorite at school. He is as glum and morose now, as if he had committed some awful crime. I wonder if he is in love?"

He looked at Jennie as he spoke, in an earnest, almost indignant manner.

"Because," continued Mr. Winne, "he is n't the sort of man to be trifled with. He has good material in him, but I imagine he would rather kill the woman he loved, than give her up to another."

"Oh!" cried Jennie, in terror, "how dreadfully you talk of killing! If that is the kind of man Reuben Harlow is, what girl would ever love him?"

"I do not know, do you?" answered Mr. Winne quietly. "By the way, Jennie, I saw you riding out the other day, in state and style, with Ross Farnham. Do you often do that?"

"Yes," said Jennie, blushing very red, "I — I — go sometimes. He is Mrs. Monroe's cousin, and he was at our house a month, last summer, and — and — " She wanted to add "I am to be his wedded wife;" but she could not. The words died on her tongue.

"Isn't he handsome?" cried Eva, impulsively. She had often seen him with Jennie. They had been in the store together to see her. That he should marry her, if he wanted to, seemed to her the most natural thing in the world. "I just think he is splendid."

"Other girls have thought so, to their cost," replied Mr. Winne. "He's a splendid scamp; that's what he is, and if I were in your place, Jennie, I would make him keep his distance. Ross Farnham has ruined many a girl's reputatation and broken her heart. If you were my sister, and he presumed to offer you any attention, I would horsewhip him."

Lucia, whose exceedingly prim and proper deportment had never challenged any man's attention, pursed her lips and looked disapproval at Jennie; but Eva felt that it was almost unkind to introduce the subject at all, and she asked, deprecatingly:

" Is he really a bad man?"

" Yes! he is known about town as a fast man. Of course, young ladies in his own set may aspire to his hand in marriage, and accept his attentions on that basis. He is handsome, fascinating, and wholly unscrupulous, with plenty of money, and all the arts and blandishments of a long experience in evil. I tell you, Jennie, you are in deadly peril, and I wonder that you do not see it, or that Mrs. Monroe allows it."

" He is a relative of Mrs. Monroe's," answered Jennie, who had hard work to keep the tears back, "and he has been very kind, and always very respectful to me."

" Perhaps he is in love; if so, why shouldn't he marry Jennie?" suggested Mrs. Winne.

"She is quite his equal, by birth and education, and he has enough money for both. There are rich men in this city who have married poor girls and given them splendid positions."

"It is not the way of his world, I suppose," said Lucia, who was eating philopœnas and breaking wish-bones with her nephews and neices. "I know one thing," she continued, significantly; "I would never accept attentions from such a man until he had signified his intentions to my friends."

"A Declaration of Independence," whispered Eva merrily into Jennie's ear; but she, poor child, was distressed beyond measure by all their insinuations. If this was to be the end of her holiday, she wished she had not come.

"They will talk differently to me when I am Ross Farnham's wife," she thought. "How I wish I could let them know of his dear love and care; but I have promised not to speak of it until he gives me permission." Aloud she said: "I am old enough now, Mr. Winne, to know right from wrong. Mr. Farnham has never given me reason to think his attentions anything but honorable. You know he associates

with the most particular ladies in the city, and
is always welcome at their homes, or to ride
or walk with them. Mrs. Monroe thinks a
great deal of him."

"And Mr. Monroe," said Mr. Winne, "for I
am told there is such a person."

"He is home so little I do not know. I
think he does not like any of his wife's friends
very much."

"Poor man!" said Mr. Winne, "I suppose he
is of the least possible account is his own household."

"Indeed you are mistaken. He turns things
over once in a while all through the house; but
he is rather quiet and patient most of the time.
Mrs. Monroe says he is a psychological something or other, and she is writing him out for a
scientific paper."

"Interesting subject," said Lucia, laughing.
"The proper study of mankind is man. Oh!
dear, I'd rather try cloaks on for a living than
be factotum to such a woman. But you need n't
learn any of her ideas, Jennie."

"I am not likely to," laughed Jennie, thankful the conversation had taken a new turn. "I

am too narrow and conservative, and behind the
age. She says I am joined to my idols of ignorance and prejudice. I expect every day to be
dismissed. Oh! what a lovely world this would
be if we all of us had money enough. I would
never want to live in any other."

"And how tired you would get," said Eva.
"Let me tell you my experience. I have an
opportunity to see the wealthiest and most elegant people in the city off guard, and oh! how
miserable and discontented they are when you
find them out."

"Tell us about them, Eva," said Jennie, nest-
ling affectionately near her. She had always
been a little afraid of Lucia, who was one of
those perfectly self-contained young ladies, who
look with tacit disapproval upon thoughtless,
impulsive girls of their own age, or near it; but
she loved bright, pleasant Eva, with her caressing ways.

"Excuse me, girls," said Mr. Winne, "I am
going to smoke a pipe of peace in the dining-
room; so you can gossip to your heart's con-
tent."

CHAPTER X.

ROMANCE AND REALITY.

"YOU must not laugh at me," began Eva, "if I moralize a little sometimes, or even become tragic; but you know I have a chance to see the world from a very different point of view from either of you, and I do not like it. I am sick of dress, tired to death of fashion, and quite ready to go back to Newton and be storekeeper and postmistress at two dollars a week; for that is all I can contrive to save here. All the rest goes for board and transient expenses. Besides, a shop-girl here is nothing more than a lay figure — a sort of talking and walking machine, while there it is rather a credit to fill the position."

"But there are some very nice young ladies in your store," said Lucia. "The principal of our school has a sister there."

"I know that they have secured positions and homes, and do not seem to mind the disadvantages; but a great many of the girls lose their self-respect and give up trying to be anybody. Bah! how I shudder sometimes as I try on a cloak or suit, and feel the hands turn-in me round and round, and hear them talk as if I were deaf, criticising my figure and appearance to my face. Old sordid Jews. You ought to see them, with such unclean hands, just loaded with diamond rings. And they would keep me standing all day. But the daughters are young and pretty, and if they want anything they get it. I must say I like to have gentlemen customers. They always let me select the cloak, and then pay the price without any haggling. One lady bought a cloak after rubbing a threadbare place in its duplicate to see if it were all wool. They say she never bought a yard of calico without chewing a piece, to see if the colors were fast."

"I would n't let her," said Jennie, indignantly.

"Then you would be reported for being impertinent. Not a week ago, a lady bought a child's cloak of me, paid for it, and left the department; but in a little while came running back, saying she had left her pocket-book. I looked everywhere, but it could not be found. She called the manager up, and told him she was positive she had left it there, and insisted that I should be searched. I told her that I had not touched it, and that I was sure she had not left it there, or I should have seen it. She got very angry, and threatened to have me arrested, when something touched her foot, and she found the pocket-book had slipped between her dress and the lining, instead of into the pocket. Instead of apologizing to me for her suspicions, she said she would never purchase of me again, because I had been impertinent, and the manager blamed me for losing her custom. There's justice and equity for you."

"I think I should have resigned my situation," said Lucia.

"No you wouldn't. You would do just as I did — cry, when you got a chance, and go right on. If you left, they wouldn't give you a reference, and you might not get another situation during the season. The girls do not mind such

6

things in the least. Sometimes a real true lady comes in; not one who is rich and patronizing, but a lady who knows just what she wants, and speaks to us as if we were human beings, with souls. Then there are some who try to be very sympathetic, and they ask us what salaries we are paid, and how we are treated, and what church or Sunday-school we attend, and want us to join the church sociables. They will be very good if we go to their particular church; but if not, we have no further notice from them. What surprises me is, that everything is so contradictory. Sometimes the richest ladies are the meanest when making purchases. They will select elegant goods, that just suit them, and then haggle over the price for an hour; and such worn out, faded out fashionable women as they are, all paint and powder, and make up, with no more expression in their faces than in a rag doll's."

"How you must dislike them," cried Jennie. "I should hate to wait on such people."

"We pity them," answered Eva. "It is such a forlorn fate to be only a walking dry-goods advertisement. And there are other women —

oh! girls, it is awful — they come there dressed like queens, in the richest of laces, and velvets, and silks, and select such elegant goods, and order them charged to Mr. A. or Mr. B., and the next day little pale Mrs. A. comes in and buys a modest, inexpensive garment, and studies over it a long time; and Mrs. B. is an invalid, and we all feel so sorry for her. Sometimes I wish I had never learned there were such wicked people in the world."

"It need make no difference with us, only to stimulate us to a better life," remarked Lucia.

"Somebody is responsible," answered Eva. "I am sorry, too, for people who make such shipwrecks of their lives. You would be, if you could hear the cruel things said about them."

"Your pity is all wasted," replied Lucia. "I should keep mine for those who are more deserving. When I find a depraved child in my school, and there are such, I can tell you, I just expel it, and so prevent its hurting twenty good children. That is the only safe plan." And Lucia looked the moral school ma'am to perfection as she spoke.

"Mrs. Monroe would tell you there were pre-

natal reasons why the child should be bad,"
said Jennie. "You ought to see the objects she
picks up and brings home. The house is like a
hospital half the time."

"Why, I thought she was an invalid," said
Lucia.

"So she is. She takes all kinds of horrid
doses, and eats five meals a day, weighing every
ounce."

"Who pays for all her philanthrophy," asked
Eva; "Mr. Monroe?"

"Well, it comes out of his pocket in the end;
but she attends meetings where they take up
collections for such purposes; and there is a
secret society, to which a number of the ladies
belong. They meet in a cellar on the West Side,
and form in procession, with black cambric robes
and masks. There is a queen — I believe Mrs.
Monroe is the queen — and they have some kind
of an order, and take solemn oaths not to tell
anything, under penalty of death. The dues
of the society are used for charitable purposes."

"Well, I don't like that Mrs. Monroe," said
Eva, decidedly. "Margaret Holmes knew a poor
seamstress who worked for her, and she says she

turned her into the street in the middle of the night for some fancied offense, and that she once had a constable in the house to arrest a poor servant girl for stealing a pair of stockings."

"Why do you stay there, Jennie," asked Lucia. "You could get a situation somewhere else for the same money."

Jennie blushed scarlet. Why *did* she stay there, sure enough? Oh! if she could only tell the girls that Ross Farnham loved her; that he had selected the ring of betrothal; that she would some day be his honored wife! Why should there be any secrecy in their love-making? He was free to choose her before the whole world.

"You ought to be with some good Christian woman, who would look upon you as a child with a soul to save. Mrs. Monroe has proved already that she is not a fit protection for any young girl," continued Lucia, warmly.

"She has lost her interest in me since she finds that I will never be a graduate of her school," said Jennie, laughing. "At any rate, I earn my bread and butter, which is more than she can do. I don't think she takes very much interest in my soul or any other soul in her dominion."

"You are fond of the pomps and vanities of this wicked world, and need the most careful restraining influences," answered Lucia.

Jennie flushed up, and the tears came into her eyes. "Pomps and vanities," she repeated, bitterly. "I have seen so much of them. I think there never was anyone who had such an appreciation of wealth, and luxury, and beautiful things, who was so completely deprived of them. Why girls, when I see beautiful ladies stepping out of elegant carriages, dressed in rich and expensive things, and everybody bowing and smiling to them, it seems just like a glimpse of Heaven, and, like Heaven, it is denied to me."

The two girls looked at her a moment in sorrowful silence. They knew of her past. They had all grown up together. They were all educated, thoughtful girls, but of the three, Jennie was the youngest and most flippant. Lucia had a great deal of mental force and culture, but her heart and feelings were regulated by a rather severe judgment. She was the first to break the transient silence.

"You are a materialist, Jennie," she said, presently. "You see only with the eyes of the flesh. If you could look deeper, with a more spiritual perception, you might behold all the deformities those silken robes cover. You might see envy, hatred, and malice lurking beneath."

"I dare say," answered Jennie, indifferently. "Unfortunately, I suffer and feel in the flesh! I am quite sure I should be a better Christian in silk and velvet than in rags, taking all accessories into consideration. I hate poverty!"

"Well, we none of us love it," said Lucia; "but I can imagine a greater poverty than any of us have ever known. A splendid poverty, that degrades and destroys its possessor."

Mr. Winne, having smoked his pipe out, here came in with a suggestion of games, and put an end to the conversation. Before doing this, he had stepped to the front door, in answer to a summons from the bell. A man stood on the steps, and a handsome carriage had stopped at the curbstone.

"Is Miss Armstrong ready to return home?" asked the man, respectfully. He was evidently the driver.

" Miss Armstrong will remain here, with her
friends, to night," answered Mr. Winne, in a
clear, decided voice. " Has Mrs. Monroe sent
for her? "

" Yes — no, sir. I had orders to call for her,"
stammered the man.

" Well, she will remain with us to-night,"
was Mr. Winne's reply, and the man shuffled
down the steps, said a few words to some one
in the carriage, and it rolled away rapidly, with
the driver in his place. Before it went, however, Mr. Winne knew whose ring it was that
for a moment flashed in the gas-light, on the
firm white hand that held the carriage door.

He did not speak of it afterwards, and Jennie
did not know how near Ross Farnham had been
to her. For that last night she was her old self
along with the girls.

CHAPTER XI.

"And the jest seldom slips
But it strikes a tender chord,
And a smile was on the lips
Of the wretch who sold his Lord!"

THE CLUB HOUSE.

HERE was a young girl who left her country home to find a situation in the city. She was beautiful and refined, had been tenderly nurtured, and her parents were very unwilling to part with her, but it seemed necessary. Weeks and months passed away and there came no word of her to her anxious friends. Finally, her old father, distracted with fear and anxiety, went to the city to look for her. He searched a long time and found many lost girls but not his own, and as all the dreadful temptations of life were revealed to him, he shuddered over the possible fate of his darling child. But one day it was revealed to him that she was dead — that she had died the day she reached the city of a sudden attack of heart disease. When satisfied of the truth the father shouted and clapped his hands for joy! People thought he had gone mad and pitied him, but he smiled at their pity and said : " To think that all the time I have been worrying and fretting about her, she was safe with the angels ! Oh, how glad her mother will be when I go home and tell her !"

I think there are many fathers who might feel as this one did, that their children would have been better cared for, had they died before the struggle for life began. Yet, as the grand lesson of triumph can only be learned through the severe discipline of trial, the world is the fittest school. They who have fallen by the wayside and perished, need no longer our help nor our tears. It is for those who have fallen and not perished, who stretch out imploring hands for our care, our sympathy in their extremity, who have loved much and suffered much, — it is for them the Christ of to-day pleads.

At this very moment the toils of sin are closing in upon some weak soul. The practiced hand of vice is leading some weary, lonely victim into the short, bright road to perdition. It is not the church nor the Sunday-school that is needed here; it is the motherly, Christian hand, irrespective of creeds or conditions, the gentle, womanly voice to warn and save.

Ross Farnham, for it was he, rode away from Mr. Winne's door in an exceedingly ill humor. He had sent regrets to a brilliant party for the purpose of escorting Jennie home, and regaling himself with an hour of her pleasant talk, and he was not accustomed to finding his wishes disregarded and obstructions in his way. The cool manner in which Mr. Winne had constituted himself Jennie's guardian, annoyed him, and he was still more vexed with himself for not having informed Jennie in advance of his intention of calling. He felt sure that she would have gone with him despite of any interference of officious friends, for he knew she was influenced by the glamour of a first love, and he sighed to himself and envied her the blissful possession.

He drove to a fashionable club house on Wabash avenue and was soon comfortably seated in the lounging room, a bottle of wine at his elbow, his feet in embroidered slippers, and a costly gold-topped meerschaum sending up clouds of perfumed smoke as he mused and looked into the glowing grate fire.

Other gentlemen lounged and smoked, and presently one came in and drew a chair close to him.

"Ah! good evening, Bates, glad to see you. What will you have, cogniac? very good. Here, you fellow," he called to a man, apparently a waiter, who was leaning at the corner of the mantel, his arms folded tightly over his chest, "Bring this gentleman's order."

The man straightened himself up, looked fixedly in the face of the speaker, flashed a glance of strange intelligence at him, and walked away.

"What a lout!" exclaimed Farnham. "He must be a new servant, and yet I am positive I have seen that cadaverous face before?"

The "fellow" soon returned, accompanied by a second waiter, who set the refreshments in place and retired. Then the first one took up his old position by the mantel, where he seemed to melt into the shadows. Neither of the gentlemen noticed what disposition he made of himself.

Mr. Bates, the senior partner of the firm of Bates & Rockwell, drank his cogniac, and between times smoked and talked with Ross Farnham. When the two had exhausted finance and politics, they turned to other and pleasanter subjects.

"I say, Farnham," remarked Bates, pleasantly, "who was the pretty little girl you were driving out on the avenue last Thursday? From the country, I should say?"

"That! let me see. Oh, she is a young lady my cousin employs as amanuensis and companion. She never gets a breath of air, and her folks were kind to me last summer when I had that infernal fall, and so I procured her the situation. She is pretty, and belongs to a good family and has been well brought up ; but they are all poor as church mice."

"Disinterested kindness," sneered Mr. Bates. "It's a bad beginning for the girl, but that's her look out. Mean to set her up like a queen, eh ?"

"I haven't decided," answered Farnham, coolly. "It's a sight of trouble, but I think in this case the game is well worth the candle."

"I feel a sort of interest," said Mr. Bates, leaning his head back, and puffing out clouds of purple smoke, while his eyes closed tranquilly, "because — hem, hem — there's a girl in the store who came from the same place. She is handsome, too, as a picture, and like all of them at first, high strung and full of notions; but she'll get over it. They all do; only Margaret Holmes — who would have thought it — has turned a bit jealous, and shows fight if I go near the Bartlett girl. I can manage, however. I have had more difficult tasks than this."

"There is one means that seldom fails," said Ross Farnham, deliberately, holding up the long, slim-necked bottle at his elbow, and looking through its half measure of crystal rosiness.

"You mean wine," answered Bates, approvingly. "Yes, that is certain, if you can only get them to taste it. Do you remember that pretty little Clara; the girl that floored half our set last winter? What a time Jack Wood had getting that girl to taste a glass of wine. She carried him to the verge of insanity with her innocent flirtations, and then coolly laughed at him for his folly. She never turned giddy in the least, till he finally, by strategy of some sort, got her to drink a glass of champagne. After that she went to destruction fast enough. She made a desperate trial to reform, and there were good women to help her, but it would n't do. She could not live without excitement and luxury. Her friends would not speak to her or own her, and she took the shortest route to perdition."

"What became of her, at last," asked Farnham, knocking the ashes from his cigar.

"Died! and by her own hand. She had an interview with Jack Wood the day before she poisoned herself, and they say she just made his hair stand up with fright at the solemn way she talked. You know he reformed, and is now the exemplary head of a family."

"I do n't see as he was to blame, particularly," said Farnham, taking a long draught from his replenished glass. "It has always been a man's privilege to ask, and a woman's to refuse. He gave her all she could ask — wealth, ease, and luxury."

"Yes; all but an honest name. I suppose there is something in that beyond our sophistry."

"An honest name! Great God!" Ross Farnham grew excited, and threw away his cigar. "How many thousands of women have dragged out their lives in penury and hardship to preserve an honest name, and what good did it ever do them? Does the world rise up, and, seeing through their pitiless make-shifts, give them of its bounty? Are they not misused, and hunted, and maligned by the very champions of virtue? Their honest wages are cut down, all avenues of employment are overfilled, the wolf is at the door — not one wolf, but an hundred — and their compensation is an honest name!"

"There is something in that we do not understand, Farnham. But we both know there are women who would starve to death by inches, till the miserable tortured body gave up its last claim, rather than surrender one iota of the spirit's purity. It is an instinct stronger than life with them. Such women cannot be tempted.

" I have missed your cowardly heart, he said."—Page 99.

You know how cruel the world is to the woman who steps aside from the narrow path of virtue. It does not ask what her temptation may be. It is of small account beside her disgrace."

"Perhaps you are right," answered Farnham, yawning. "I know this; they have the worst of it here; but if there is a hereafter, and I for one believe there is, there will be a heavy score to settle against us. I am going to my punishment with my eyes open, for I never believed that, of two responsible human beings, with equal attributes in the sight of Heaven, one was to have all the privileges and the other all the penalties. If I go scot free in this world, I shall have my turn in the next; but if a class of human beings are born into the world preordained to destruction, I am but the instrument of fate."

"Well, I should never add hypocrisy to my other sins. I am not a praying member in a church, and *you* know what my home life has been. I should never use unfair means to induce any girl to place herself under my protection. There are women, respectably married, in this city to-day, who can testify to that. It is a

7

question that involves an immense amount of speculative thought, and no one has ever reached a satisfactory solution."

"Then it is useless for us to begin. Now here is a girl," Farnham spoke in a low tone, " who is as lovely as a Grecian model. She has education, refinement, and, so far, good principles, though no fixed character. She was dissatisfied with her country home and her farmer lover, and the poverty of her surroundings. She has an unsatiated thirst for the beautiful. She admires all the precious things wealth can bestow. She wants luxury, diamonds, and cashmere, velvets and laces, leisure instead of toil, and by G— she shall have them!

He had spoken in a low tone, but the man standing motionless among the shadows heard every word. Taking something from the breast of his coat, he again folded his arms, and stood motionless, as before.

"She does not expect you to marry her?" asked Mr. Bates. "Now, in my case, there can be no delusion of that sort. With you it is only natural that any girl you might honor with your attention should aspire to a matrimonial right to your name."

"I shall never marry," said Farnham. "I know the world too well. Jennie Armstrong may look forward to an ultimatum of marriage, and there will be time enough to undeceive her. She is madly in love with me now."

"LIAR!" It was not the word that reverberated through the room, but the shot that followed it, and brought Ross Farnham to his feet, with his right arm hanging helpless by his side. The man who had stood by the mantel took a step forward. "I have missed your cowardly heart," he said; but that moment Ross Farnham raised his left hand, in which something glittered. A second report cleft the air, and the man dropped, with a dull sound, on the floor.

A crowd instantly gathered. Some one lifted the limp form, and found life. The man was shot through the lungs, and death must be inevitable; yet he was still breathing.

. There was no paper nor memoranda to declare who he was, or whence he came. He was not a servant, and had never been seen in the club-rooms before that evening. He was supposed to be some gentleman's attendant, as his style of dress was neither that of a servant nor a gentleman. Who was he, and what was his object in assaulting Mr. Farnham?

Meanwhile the man lay prostrate and unconscious. The pistol which he had aimed at his enemy's heart was still clasped tightly in his hand; his eyes were closed, his face was pallid, and his breath came in great gasps. In this state he was lifted to an improvised stretcher and carried off to a remote hospital until such time as he should die, or get well enough to be be indicted for murder.

If Ross Farnham knew him in that moment, he made no sign. A silken handkerchief had been bound tightly about his own arm. It was only a flesh wound, after all, and he had denied to everybody who asked him any knowledge of the man, or of his intentions. There were plenty of people present who could conceive of sufficient reason why a man of his reputation should be in danger of an attack upon his life, but they considered silence their best policy.

The next morning the daily papers published glowing accounts of Mr. Farnham's bravery in repulsing an assassin, and relegated the would-be murderer to certain punishment as soon as his wounded lungs should become sufficiently healed. At this knowing people smiled, and remarked that "Law and justice were two different institutions."

CHAPTER XII.

MRS. MONROE'S HUSBAND.

HE was known to the world as such, his identity being completely swallowed up in that of his wife. How could it be otherwise? He was not president of the B. W. A. S., nor leader of a secret society, that had processions in a cellar, and wore paper cambric robes, nor treasurer of a Dorcas sewing club, that did everything but sew, nor correspondent of a political reform organ. He had never been invited to deliver addresses to the working women, nor solicit aid for the unfortunate, or for the reform of the fallen. He was merely an appendage to Mrs. Monroe, furnishing her with a frescoed roof, paying her bills, and reading her name in a newspaper report as the agitator of some new scheme for a hospital or a prison. He had never read her book on co-operative housekeeping, but he thought almost

any housekeeping might be an improvement on
the home plan. He was so accustomed to see
his parlor occupied by spectacled women, carry-
ing rolls of manuscript, petitions, and docu-
ments, that when he found it empty he bowed to
the chairs, from mere force of habit. He loved
children, but it was one of his wife's idiosyn-
crasies not to have any, while so many superfluous children were struggling for a place. She
had adopted one of those superfluous children
once, in a fit of enthusiasm, and for three months
of its life the baby was fêted and feasted. It
slept in a rosewood crib, kindly loaned by Mrs.
Judge Smythe, was dressed in contributed laces
and finery, and its sleeves were tied up with gold
chains. Then a re-action set in, and it was
bundled off to the nurse, who bribed the cook to
take care of it at night, and so it caught its death
of cold.. There was a splendid funeral, which all
the friends attended, and a poor relation, who
had fallen into disfavor, spitefully remarked that
half what that casket cost would have kept her
in coals for the winter!

The evening that Jennie spent at Mr. Winne's
Mr. Monroe found himself alone with his wife,

a *tête-à-tête* she always avoided, and that he seldom enjoyed. He was a thin, slender man, with a nervous mouth, half concealed by a chestnut moustache. He looked just the sort of man to be moulded by a woman. He had not force of character enough to emphasize his own opinions. He preferred to do right, and live up to his own convictions, but was willing to sacrifice principles to peace. His wife had frequently told him that he ought to have married a Dora Copperfield — a home body, a pleasant sort of idiot, and how fervently he sometimes wished that he had.

He was visiting in his wife's room, now, where he always felt like an intruder, although he reposed nightly, when at home, beneath the embroidered quilt, with a wax Cupid dangling within an inch of his nose. On this night his heart yearned for companionship, and he sought his wife, with the forlorn hope that she might care to amuse and entertain him. He found her reading a statistical looking paper, cutting out sentences, and marking annotations on the margin. She was handsomely dressed, and looked queenly and imposing.

"Maria," he commenced, throwing himself into a chair hung with rich embroidery, "what are you reading?"

"An article headed 'What to do with our daughters.' I find some excellent things in it, and I mean to write a paper on the subject and read it at our next maternity meeting."

"We have n't any daughters. I did not know that you cared about such matters."

"Other people have daughters, Mr. Monroe," answered his wife, loftily.

"Yes; and it is about them I would like to speak. I saw that kitchen girl of yours — what is her name — flaunting down street, when I came in, and I think she needs a little motherly care."

Mrs. Monroe laid down her paper. "I 'll turn her out of the house to-morrow. I told her I should if she went out another evening. To think what I rescued that girl from, and now this is her gratitude."

"You cannot expect to have all the virtues for three dollars a week. I do not see how it would improve matters, either, to turn her out on the streets. You might easily interest yourself enough in her to know where she is, and how she passes her time. I suppose philanthropy at home is as necessary as in charitable institutions."

"Did you come up here on purpose to say that, Mr. Monroe?" asked his wife, in a hard, disagreeable voice. In talking to her husband, there was none of that effusiveness that characterized her with acquaintances. "Because, if you take so much interest in Sarah, you might look after her yourself."

The man did not resent the insult. Naturally affectionate and home-loving, though warped aside by adverse influences, he longed, to-night, with a homesickness that was pain, for the company of a congenial nature.

"Will you play Bezique?" he asked, presently, as his wife resumed her reading.

She consented ungraciously, and so an hour passed, and the clock struck nine.

"Where is Jennie?" asked Mr. Monroe, putting the cards in the cribbage box.

"She has been spending the day at Mr. Winne's, with some friends. I expect she will stay all night, unless Ross should call for her."

"Maria," said Mr. Monroe, gravely, bending over the table that separated him from his wife, "Do you know what you are doing? You are helping that girl to her ruin."

His wife threw down the paper she had resumed. "I do not understand," she said, angrily. "I have rescued her from poverty and obscurity, and given her the means of helping herself and her parents. If that should prove her ruin you cannot blame me."

"At whose suggestion did you do it? Not mine. You engaged that girl to come here as a sort of factotum, because Ross Farnham took a fancy to her last summer. You know what he is; and yet you throw her in his way, and give her no warning. If she falls, the price of her dishonor is your lawful wages."

"She is not a child," answered his wife, an angry light gleaming in her eyes. "She must take her chances with the rest of the world. I have advised and instructed her, and told her she might make herself a name in some intellectual way. She is well educated, and has read a great deal, and I could forward her interests in many ways; but she has no taste for such high pursuits. Now there is my lecture on physical culture. I have offered to let her read it at different places — she has really a fine voice — but she has no self reliance. There is nothing progressive about her. She has been taught at her mother's apron strings, and has just one set of ideas."

"It is a pity she had not staid there. Her beauty and ignorance are both against her here. You women who are always meddling with reforms never use the material at hand. How many of you interest yourselves in the souls under your own roof? It is the unknown heathen you labor to convert."

Mr. Monroe seldom denounced his wife's theories as bitterly as he did to-night. He had married her at a venture, and lost. That there were circumstances in her past life not to her credit, he did not care to know. He knew too much as it was. He was master in his own house in only one way. He paid the bills, and the servants run the domestic machinery on the co-operative plan; that is, they co-operated to see that their respective households did not want.

As he went out of her room, preparatory to putting on his overcoat to spend a social evening elsewhere, his wife looked after him. " How I hate you! " was the thought uppermost in her mind. Before his footsteps had died away on the pavement, she was writing an article on the tyranny of marriage, which other dissatisfied women should read and applaud.

She did not care where nor how he spent his time, so that he did not interfere with her selfishly lazy life. She felt no moral obligation to make his home happy and comfortable, and to minister to his wants with her own hands. Necessity had not driven her to her present pursuits for bread and butter. A wholesome course of physical labor would soon have cured her of any tendency to invalidism. She had elected herself as champion of her sex, and yet it was true that she had turned a young and thoughtless girl into the streets at midnight, because Mr. Monroe, returning late from a club supper, had met her in the hall, and attempted to kiss her! It was a very reprehensible act, no doubt, in one denied legitimate caresses, but the punishment for it should have been visited on him alone.

CHAPTER XIII.

JUDAS IN PETTICOATS.

THE morning after Thanksgiving day Jennie awoke, and found that it was very late. The other two girls had risen without disturbing her, their time being limited to certain hours; and when she went down to the breakfast room she found Mrs. Winne alone with the children, lingering over the toast and coffee, and looking very much annoyed. When Jennie entered, with excuses for her late appearance, Mrs. Winne handed her the morning paper.

"You will find some news there," she said coldly. "I think you are interested in the matter. Who do you think the man is that Ross Farnham shot last night?"

Jennie heard but one sentence. "Ross Farnham! Shot! Last night!"—the room spun round, and all the world turned dark. The color

left her cheeks and lips, and she stood staring
blankly at the paper in her hand.

"Do n't look so dreadfully," exclaimed Mrs.
Winne, "there is n't anybody killed, but there
might have been. Read that paper, and see."

"Who was it tried to kill Ross, Mrs. Winne?"
asked Jennie, with white lips.

"Albert said it was Reuben Harlow. He felt
dreadfully about it, Jennie, and blamed you
pretty severely; but I do n't see how you can
help them falling in love with you."

Jennie read the notice as well as she could,
and saw that no one was killed — at least that
Ross was not — then she flung the paper on the
table, and began to cry.

"I wish Reuben Harlow would mind his own
affairs. What business has he to watch a gentleman like Mr. Farnham, and call him to account? If he had killed him, it would have
been murder! I hate Reuben, and he might
know it by this time. How dared he follow me
to the city!"

"Oh, Jennie, do be careful!" suggested Mrs.
Winne, who, from never having any of her own,
rather enjoyed sensations in other people's love

affairs. "I do n't believe Ross Farnham has any idea of marrying you, and you ought not to accept his attentions. I wish you had never gone to Mrs. Monroe's. If I were you I would go home again."

"Home!" Jennie shut her eyes and conjured up a vision of the old, unpainted, tumble-down house, the dilapidated farm, and the days that were all like Sundays, with the toil-worn pair who could give her nothing but their love, and to whom life had been one perpetual rainy day. No! She could not go home!

Mrs. Winne gave her some good advice at parting, for which she thanked her, and then set out for Mrs. Monroe's. The day was bright and cold, the air pure and invigorating, but Jennie walked steadily along, her eyes bent on the ground. She was taking a practical look at life, and trying to expunge all the blue and rose color from its neutral gray. As she walked along thus she looked prettier and more bewitching than ever. Not the most studied coquetry could have made her face so attractive as the pretty air of perplexity that drew her cherry lips into a delicious Cupid's bow, and arched her dark and dainty eyebrows into a sinuous line, and sent the long, quivering lashes downward, like pencillings, on the clear red of her cheeks. A coarse, bright shawl was wrapped about her slender form, one end falling over her shoulder. Her plain straw hat had a red wing jauntily set in the velvet band, and, with all the lights and colors of her dress, and of herself, she resembled some rare tropical bird. So thought Ross Farnham, as he looked after her, his heart full of admiration and — would you call it love? She had passed him so close that her fluttering silken hair had brushed his arm —the arm carried in a sling — but she either did not or would not see him. He turned and looked after her for a moment with a surprised air, and then, with a rapid motion or two, was at her side.

"Miss Armstrong," lifting his hat, as she turned at the sound of his voice, "are you so pre-occupied that you cannot see your friends?"

Jennie looked at him without any of her usual pretty embarrassment; but the sight of his wounded arm touched her visibly. Her heart beat so violently she could with difficulty speak.

"I am in a great hurry," she said. "It is

8

late, and Mrs. Monroe will need me; besides, Mr. Farnham, I have seen the paper, and — and my friends think —— " then, suddenly changing to an anxious, natural tone, " Was it Reuben Harlow who shot you, Mr. Farnham?"

" I presume it was," he replied, indifferently. " I did not notice the fellow particularly."

" Was he — was he killed?" in a horror-stricken voice.

" Killed! no! no! not half so bad as that. I will see that he wants nothing, since you are so interested in him; and I assure you his hurt is not more serious than mine. Only no one cares in the least that I am hurt," and he sighed despondently.

" Your friends will all care, Mr. Farnham, but I have known Reuben Harlow since I was a little child, and I cannot bear to think he should lose his life for me; I am not worth it."

Ross Farnham thought she was worth that, and a great deal more, as he looked into her shy, brown eyes, filled with tears of the deepest contrition. A sudden impulse came over him to release himself from the bonds of his set, and own her before the world as his chosen wife. But the demon of pride held him back, and a more cruel demon whispered its evil counsel. He held out his hand to Jennie, and whispered one charmed word, "Darling!"

How often, in the last few weeks, she had blushed a celestial red at this tender word. How it had thrilled her poor little deluded heart with a passionate delight; but now she shook her head sadly. She must not let him say it any more.

"Mr. Farnham," she began in a dignified voice, "my friends blame me very much for what has happened, and think I have not been particular enough in remembering my position. I do not care in the least for Reuben Harlow, or — or any one else in that way; and I know I ought not to accept attentions from any gentleman, unless——" she stopped and looked at him pitifully, "unless as his promised wife. I am a poor girl, and must make my own way in the world, and not give anyone the chance to say cruel or unkind things about me."

"Who has dared to say unkind things? Let me know who dares even to hint at any such calumny," he exclaimed in a fierce whisper, that made Jennie's foolish heart thrill with joy.

"They blame me for what happened last night; but I did not even know, until then, that Reuben Harlow was in the city. Tell me, Mr. Farnham, how did it happen. What was the quarrel about?"

"I shall not tell you one word if you talk in that way. Call me Ross; not that cold Mr. Farnham. There is nothing to tell, really, only that Mr. Harlow did me the great honor of being jealous of me, and intended then and there to put it out of my power to love anybody. I merely defended myself by a return shot. Would you have cared, Jennie, if I had been killed? Answer me truly, darling."

He looked into her troubled eyes with a tenderness that was magnetizing. She felt the influence of that look, and hastened to break it.

"Killed! Oh, Ross! What am I saying. I cannot bear to think that any life might have been lost for such a foolish, giddy girl. What would my father and mother say? I can never be anything to Reuben Harlow, nor to anyone else. I am a poor girl, working for my living, and I need to be more careful than those who have home and friends to care for them. My family have always been honorable and respectable, if they are poor."

Ross Farnham thought he had never admired her so much as at that moment. Her eyes were filled with the sweet dew of humility, and when she repeated the assertion, " I am a poor girl," she looked up at him with a pride that rivalled his own. Almost he was ashamed of himself. Almost he determined to let this little wild flower bloom unplucked, or else to wear it in his bosom, that all the world might see. Then the hydra-headed serpent of selfishness reared itself in his sight, and his spasm of goodness was over.

" You are tired and depressed," he said, kindly. " Do not let any narrow - minded, conservative set of people sway you into their narrow groove of thought and action. As for myself, I am willing to die in your service. I cherish this wounded arm as a soldier does his medal of honor. Am I presumptuous! Good bye, till I see you again." He lifted his hat, looked at her with a half sad smile, and turned back at his cousin's door.

It was all very fine acting, but how was Jennie to know? She had never been to a theatre, and by no comparison could decide the real from the ideal. When Ross Farnham looked at her in that way, her world was conquered.

Mrs. Monroe was not exactly in good humor when Jennie reached home. The B. W. A. S. correspondence had got into a snarl. The treasurer had reported fourteen cents on hand, after a threé o'clock lunch which the society had indulged in, but on demand, it was found to be only eleven cents. Three had been feloniously abstracted. Every member looked at every other member with suspicion, when the affair was known, and sent in a four-page letter of remonstrance to the President. All the letters had arrived in one mail that morning, while the president was taking her tea and toast in bed, and they had literally overwhelmed her. Jennie tried to sort out the letters and put them in shape, expecting every moment that Mrs. Monroe would allude to the account in the morning papers. She did not, however, for the sufficient reason that she knew nothing about it. If Mr. Monroe had seen the intelligence, he had not thought it worth while to enlighten his wife.

" You can take the tray out, Jennie," said Mrs. Monroe, "and hand me the paper. Raise the curtain a little. Tell Esther I would like a sago pudding for lunch, and see what that giddy Sarah is about. You can answer those letters this afternoon. If I feel well enough I will try to attend the maternity meeting at Mrs. Field's. You might get out my seal-skin cloak and cap, and tell Horace to be ready with the carriage at two."

Jennie withdrew and quickly fulfilled her orders. She was in her own room, when a loud scream from Mrs. Monroe startled her, though she instantly divined what it meant. Her heart throbbed guiltily as she entered the room and saw Mrs. Monroe looking very white and stern, her finger placed on a paragraph in the paper.

"Girl!" she exclaimed, as Jennie stood silent and abashed before her, "see what you have done! I hope you are satisfied with the mischief you have wrought. It is not enough that Ross Farnham has rescued you from poverty and obscurity. but you must be the means of nearly costing him his life, with your baby face and childish ways. Who is this man who tried to shoot him down like an assassin?"

"It is Reuben Harlow. He has been in the city for some time, but I did not know it till last night. He has no right to watch me, or any one who is seen in my company. I don't see how you can blame me, Mrs. Monroe, for what has happened."

"I do blame you for always thrusting yourself into notice when Mr. Farnham is here. I have tried my best to make you think of higher objects in life than the admiration and attention of gentlemen. Let me tell you, Ross Farnham will never marry you. He will wring all the sweetness from your life, and throw it away an utter wreck. If you have learned to love him, unlearn it as soon as you can. You will have no recompense in this world. I wish you had never seen him."

Ah! if she had only told Jennie her own story then — told it, not in bitterness and anger, but in womanly sorrow and humility, what after hours of anguish might have been spared her.

Jennie answered none of the accusations

against her, but went about her duties for the
day without a word. Her heart was full to
overflowing, and she saw everything through a
mist of tears. "He loves me not; he loves me
not, and I have given my heart to him beyond
recall," she kept thinking over and over. She
was glad when Mrs. Monroe was dressed and
ready for the maternity meeting. "I wonder,"
she thought, "if they will discuss me among
them."

. She went back up stairs into the empty rooms
and began putting them in order. They were
full of carved beauty and embroidered sentiment,
but among them a human soul was being rent
and torn, and it was valued the least of anything there. "What shall I do; what shall I
do?" the girl was saying to herself repeatedly,
as she folded splendid robes and laid them away.
It seemed, already, as if disgrace had overtaken
her. She finished her duties, and then· threw
herself into a chair and tried to think.

Mrs. Monroe had a very comfortable time at
the maternity meeting. She prayed fervently
for "the dear children committed to our care,"
and was very gracious to everybody. She did

not go to the office for her husband, but on her way home she picked up her cousin, just parting from some ladies who had gushed sympathetically over him. They had a long confidential talk before they reached home, and there were traces of angry tears on Mrs. Monroe's enamelled checks when she stepped from her carriage. Ross did not go into the house. He gave his cousin's coachman a direction, and drove away. They stopped near the corner of Eighteenth street and Wabash avenue.

"You can return home," said Mr. Farnham, placing a liberal *douceur* in the man's hand. He walked on until he came to a handsome marble front house, which looked as if it were shut up and forsaken, all the shutters being closed and the bars dropped. He rang the silver-handled bell, and, after a very brief delay, the door was opened by a small boy, black and sleek.

"Is your mistress in?" asked Mr. Farnham, following him into the darkened parlor.

"Yes, sir; missis is up stairs."

"Then give her this," and he laid his card in the outstretched ebony palm.

The boy grinned, backed out of the room, and

with three bounds mounted the stately staircase
and delivered his message.

Ross Farnham, meanwhile, made himself perfectly at home. He drew aside the costly
wrought lace curtains from the windows, and,
opening one, turned back the closed shutters.
Then he took a critical survey of the apartment.
It was faultlessly splendid in all its elegant ap-
pointments, velvet carpets of rose and wood color,
gold-leaf and drab on the walls, mosaic tables,
mirrors, pictures of rarest beauty and value, luxurious chairs and divans, no two alike, and rare
and costly *bric-à-brac* everywhere. Not a speck
of dust nor a sign of disorder was visible, nor yet
any of the stiffness or newness of elegant fur-
nishings. In an arch at the end of the room
were three exquisite statues of Faith, Hope, and
Charity, and upon a background of Cardinal red
velvet hung Thorvaldsen's Night and Morning
in *bas-relief*.

A slight rustle at the door announced the mistress of all this grandeur. Farnham was exam-
ining a new engraving on the centre table. He
lifted his eyes a moment, nodded coolly, and
went on with his inspection.

The woman who entered was about twenty-eight years old, tall and slender, and dark, with flashing black eyes and stormy brows. Her cheeks were redder than nature intended them to be, and her dress was too elaborate for a home toilet. Her features were small and regular, but worn by care or dissipation. She started when she saw the wounded arm.

"Have you come for me to nurse you," she asked, in a voice not inharmonious, but lacking culture. "I saw this morning you were in trouble. Who is it about this time?"

"That is what I came to talk about, Helen; I felt sure that I could trust you."

"Don't be too sure," said the woman mockingly, while a sudden gleam lightened her bad, dark eyes. "You have not been here for a long time; but I know where you have been."

"Do you? Then it is unnecessary for me to tell you. I came here on business to-day. Do you care to renew the lease of this house, or shall I let it to another tenant?"

"You did not come here to-day to ask me that, Ross; you are trying to frighten me, but it is of no use. We have too many mutual interests at stake to quarrel."

"I am glad you think so, Helen. Now listen, and I will tell you the reason of my present visit. You will find it to your interest to serve me faithfully."

They held a long conference, the nature of which these pages will in due time reveal.

CHAPTER XIV.

A FEATHER HE DID NOT WEAR.

EVA had left her situation. It happened in this way: Mr. Bates had decided in his own mind that something definite must be done to forward his wicked project in regard to Eva, therefore the morning after his encounter with Ross Farnham he decided to approach the subject as nearly as he dared, by inviting her to accompany him to the theatre in the evening. A new play, by some local genius, was attracting attention, and Eva had unguardedly expressed, in his hearing, a wish to see it. Taking an opportunity, when he had some orders to give concerning the stock, he invited her, in a whispered communication that caused her cheeks to redden consciously, for she felt that the eyes of the other employees were upon her. She never could tell what answer she did make, but

it must have been construed into an affirmative
one, for he said, in the same cautious monotone:

"I will be there with the carriage at eight, or
a little earlier. You can leave the store at three,
to-day;" and he passed on, leaving the bewildered
girl in a maze of doubt and surprise. She saw
the other girls looking and smiling, some with
envious shrugs and side glances of mocking
disdain. Help it she could not, but it seemed to
her as if some barrier of innocence had been
thrown down, since last she looked at them, and
her cheeks flamed as if she were already guilty.
Margaret Holmes was not in the store that day.
She had a cold, and sore throat, and had staid at
home to take care of herself, protesting against
the enforced idleness. She dreaded being absent
from the store for one day, feeling that Eva
needed her protection every moment. She had
become very fond of the young girl, who was
giving her whole heart to her work, enduring its
toil and nameless hardships for the sake of the
dear ones at home, and she vowed to herself that
not the shadow of harm should come to her
while she lived to avert it.

Margaret had grown very restless as the time

came near for Eva's return. A forlorn woman, who had been trying to get a situation for at least a year, and had baited the wolf at her door with bits of sewing, odd jobs of nursing, and copying, a strange combination, had been in, with a flushed face, to say that she had secured a job for the winter, of making waterproofs at forty cents each.

"Why, I would have taken them at twenty-five cents," she said, "rather than not have had them. I can make two a day easily, by sitting up nights at the button-holes. I declare I had to come and tell you of my good luck. The Lord does seem to remember us sometimes."

Margaret Holmes smiled sadly as the rusty alpaca dress of her visitor vanished from sight.

"I wonder," she mused aloud, "if He does care that we suffer, and lack every good thing in life, and if it is really true that He sees our compensation, and knows that our sorrow endures only for a day? I am sure, when I was a girl, all my impulses were good, and I had such a sincere belief that God would take care of me, until" — then she clasped her hands over her thin face, flushed with fever — "until it was

too late ! Oh God, how true that homely sentence is, that our lives are made up of just two
regrets: 'I wish that I had, and I wish that I
had n't.' I wonder, if I had my life to live over
again, if I should do any better !"

Just then a pleasant looking little woman,
whose room was next door, looked in, and asked
Margaret if she felt better. "I thought your
room-mate was here," she said. "I met her
early this afternoon, and supposed she was
coming home to sit with you."

"Met Eva ! I think you must be mistaken.
She cannot leave the store until six."

"Oh no, there was no mistake. She was
walking very slowly, and looking about her; but
she did not notice me. I observed her particularly, she had such a lovely color."

Margaret Holmes said no more, and the caller
went into her own room. When the door had
closed and she was alone, Margaret sank back on
the lounge, where she had lain all day, and
clasped her hands in perplexity.

"What has happened to take her out of the
store this afternoon ? Has he taken advantage
of this one day's absence to further his infernal

9

schemes? He shall not! He shall not! I have sworn to my own soul to save this girl from the fate that, sooner or later, is offered to them all! It is time she was here now; is that her step?"

Yes, it was. Eva came in with an excitement in her manner that was not natural. She asked Margaret how her headache was, without looking at her; moved her things restlessly from one place to another, and finally went down to supper, without alluding to the fact that she had left the store earlier than usual.

Margaret asked no questions. She felt hurt at this first want of confidence in her, surprised and grieved at Eva's changed manner, and distressed beyond measure at what it implied; but she deemed it wisest to be silent for the present.

Eva merely made a pretense of supper, to compose her mind over the events of the day. She had left the store at three, and walked all the way home, first, however, loitering through the principal streets, which were gay with elegantly dressed ladies. The stores were trimmed for the holidays, and presented a very bright appearance. It was like an enchanted city to

Eva, looking at it with work-a-day eyes. She passed the gorgeous theatre, and wondered how it looked within when all the splendid chandeliers were alight. If only she had said no; yet what harm could there be in going just once? She was sure she could take care of herself. She knew that a very nice young lady had accompanied Mr. Bates quite lately, and as his wife was absent no one thought anything of it. She longed to see a play. Margaret would be very angry, but why let her know? She was not compelled to do as Margaret Holmes wanted her to; besides Margaret was prejudiced. She would go just this once, and write all about it to her good, sensible mother the next day. She had not time to arrive at any decision before she had to return to her room to get ready. She was glad that Margaret was asleep, and moved about very lightly as she changed her dress and ribbons, and put on her best hat. She hoped to steal out softly and not awaken the invalid, but as she opened the door, a hand was laid on her shoulder compelling her to turn. Margaret's face, white and set, confronted her.

"Child!" she said, in low, husky tones, "you

are going to do some wrong thing this night.
What is it?"

Eva had intended to put her off, or if obliged
to reveal anything, to be hard and defiant; but
she could not dissemble as she looked into that
face, behind which an awful shadow seemed
lurking — the shadow of death! — it was so
white and solemn! She led Margaret back to
the lounge, and kneeling beside her, pillowed the
hot head on her arms, while she told her, with
sobs of feeling, the truth!

When she had finished Margaret Holmes arose
from the lounge. "Give me your hat and shawl,"
she said firmly; "and your blue veil, quick! We
are the same height. Here, help me arrange the
veil. Now, child, pray God I may be permitted
to be your deliverer."

She passed out of the room, and down the
stairs to the hall door. As she opened it she
saw a carriage drawn under the lamps. She
moved quickly toward it, the cold air cutting her
thin frame like a knife.

"I was so afraid you would not come. How
did you manage?" asked a well-known voice
within. So far the disguise answered.

The driver held the door open, and the veiled and disguised figure sprang in, and the next moment the horses moved rapidly away.

"You are shivering," said Mr. Bates, for it was he; "let me wrap this carriage robe around you. You were so good to come. Did Margaret Holmes suspect anything?"

He had not considered it necessary to remove his arm after encircling the trembling form with the furry robe, and he now endeavored to turn the unwilling face toward him, and was trying to look through the obscurity of the blue veil, when a feverish hand withdrew it, and a worn, white face confronted him. Thrown entirely off his guard, he uttered a fierce oath and glared angrily at her; then he muttered sullenly:

"You are determined, it seems, to cross my path. I do not know what your reasons are, but I shall put it out of your power to watch me any further; I will suffer no spy on my actions, you, least of all. I require your services no longer in any capacity."

"Defy me if you choose," answered Margaret, firmly; "I am what you made me. It seems you do not fear me any longer; for myself I ask nothing; I accept my dismissal; but if you ever dare to offer your wicked attentions to this young girl, whom I have saved to-night from villainy she does not dream of, I will denounce you to the world you deceive and the family you so wickedly wrong. You need to fear me; my ruined life shall haunt you yet, a dark spectre of your own conjuring. Something tells me that these are my last words to you; remember them when you come to die!"

She stopped the carriage, got out, and walked home, with a weariness of body she did not notice, and a pain at her heart that was like mortal agony, as she entered the portals of the Home. When she left it again it was for a longer journey.

CHAPTER XV.

ON THE BRINK.

WHEN Jennie had finished the duties devolving upon her in the absence of Mrs. Monroe, she went into her own little room and sat down to think — to try to think, would be nearer the truth. Her mind was in a maze of perplexity and trouble, and she longed for some help to enable her to walk in the right way. She had never been taught to rely upon herself. The world had been to her as a sealed book hitherto; now it had opened at one of its brightest pages, where love was the glowing inscription. Must hers be the hand to close it again? Must she give up this beautiful, blessed vision, and go back to the dreary farmhouse, to long monotonous years of toil, and end her dreams as her mother's had ended, in weariness and disappointment? Then she pictured herself as Ross Farnham's wife — his loving and beloved wife — with the right to receive and return his caresses, and to claim his affection before the whole world. She had loved him since the hour she first met him; loved him with that wild, all-absorbing love that only a few women, thank Heaven, are capable of cherishing. In her eyes he was as a God among other men. She believed him good and true. Of the dark and sinful by-ways of life Jennie knew nothing; she had only a nameless sort of horror for vice, which was not clearly comprehended.

She had performed to-day the highest act of heroism of which her undeveloped nature was capable, when she spoke as she did to Ross Farnham. It had cut her to the heart at the time, and it hurt her now to think of it. That she could have been cruel and unkind to him, when he bore a wounded arm in her defense! He had so often told her he loved her, not in any mere complimentary terms, but in low, sweet words of burning eloquence, uttered at stolen opportunities, and by so many of those tender caressing ways which are the small change of the agents of sin, or the true declarations of a loving heart; but of marriage he had not spoken; that was her own inference. She wondered why Mrs. Monroe had changed so in her treatment of her; why she had grown cold, and capricious, and often very unkind.

She leaned her head wearily on her hand — where should she turn for help? Then came over her, like an inspiration, the memory of what her mother had done when torn by doubts and perplexities; she had prayed. Prayer, with youth, seems more of a pleasant habit than a necessity. Youth and health are all-sufficient until the dark days come to turn the longing hearts heavenward. Jennie thought that God must help her if she asked it of him; she remembered when a little girl, she had prayed once for a doll, and it came; she did not reflect that earthly ears had heard her petition, and earthly love supplied the want. Now she threw herself on her knees, and prayed with all her heart, and yet the spirit of her prayer was, " Not Thy will but mine be done."

Is there any help in prayer! Yes! there is strength and peace. That the Infinite God will change any of His plans for your asking or for mine is hard to believe; we have all pleaded to retain our treasures, even while they passed beyond our grasp; we ask God to take care of us here, and He does not, but just where our imperfect work is dropped He takes it up and completes it in His time and way. We see only the sorrow and the sin; He sees the compensation. More, we know not.

Jennie arose from her knees, comforted in some vague way; then she thought of the little book she had promised her mother to read, and she went down on her knees again and searched her trunk for it. It was not to be found, and after a little time she remembered losing it as she left home. She hoped her mother would never know of her defection in the matter.

She was still sitting there, still thinking —. trying to work out some rule of conduct, when Mrs. Monroe returned, very tired, very cross, and with an unusual amount of headache and indisposition. Jennie hurried to assist her, wiping away all traces of tears and worry from her own fair face. She had many gentle, fondling ways, and although she could not offer any real demonstrations of love to her mistress, there were times when her heart yearned for sympathy, and went out in silent caresses, manifested chiefly in a tender manner, which Mrs. Monroe accepted as homage due to her, sometimes in silence, occasionally with a patronizing remark.

It was a pity that her beautiful theory of maternity, as promulgated on the platform and in print, could not have been illustrated now, upon this young girl standing on the brink of ruin. Will she warn and save her? Will God permit this girl's soul to be caught in the snare?

Upon this evening, Mrs. Monroe was more cross, more capricious, and more disagreeable than usual, and seemed bent upon a quarrel with some one. Jennie concluded that the maternity meeting had not been altogether a success, as she sought an anodyne where she often found it, in a colorless liquid with a pungent odor, and Jennie, having laid away the seal-skin cloak and its appurtenances, went back to her room and closed the door, more depressed than ever. She was busy at some sewing, when Mrs. Monroe's bell rang, and she noticed that it was growing dark. She found her mistress wrapped in her usual, toga — a robe-de-chambre — and lying on a lounge, with a bottle of ammonia in her hand.

"Come here," she said, as Jennie came into the room, "I have something to say to you."

She did not seem in any hurry to say it, but soaked her handkerchief in camphor and applied it to her head; then she resumed the ammonia. Jennie waited, with the feelings of a naughty child who expects a chiding.

"I am going to send you away," exclaimed Mrs. Monroe, breaking the silence abruptly, "and I think it best you should go at once. Here are ten dollars, all I owe you; I suppose you can stop with your friends until you find another place."

"Send me away!" repeated Jennie, mechanically. "Oh! Mrs. Monroe, what have I done that you send me out of your house without a moment's notice? I have tried to please you, and you have said you liked me, and now, oh, what will my mother say!"

"I cannot help it," answered Mrs. Monroe. She had reasons for not wishing to prolong the interview. "Mr. Monroe thinks I keep too much help, and you are quite too vain and giddy to stay with me. I cannot have a scene," she added, her voice rising to a shriek; "my nerves are not strong. You choose to set people talking about you, and must bear the consequences. I have tried to do my duty by you. Go right to your friends before it is any darker. You can send for your trunk to-morrow."

Jennie fell down beside the lounge, and clasped the large, white, cruel-looking hands, heavy with jewelled rings, in her small, dimpled ones.

"Oh, dear Mrs. Monroe," she pleaded, "do let me stay with you; I will work for nothing. At least, let me stay till I can find another place; I have no friends to stay with, even to-night; what would the Winnes think of me? I will not be any more trouble to you if you will let me stay."

"You are distressing me dreadfully," answered the champion of her sex, loosing her hands and pushing back the kneeling girl. "I consider it my duty to send you away for your own good; now go at once, or I'shall call for Esther to compel you to leave."

"You need not," said Jennie quickly, rising to her feet. "Proud, cruel woman! I will never ask another favor of you, and I hope God may deal with you as you have dealt with me this night."

She went into her room, and was soon ready to depart. As she passed down the stairs she heard Esther and Sarah laughing in the kitchen, and turned to go down and say good-bye to them, but their probable questions dismayed her. "What could I tell them," she thought; "that I am turned out of the house. But what is it for?"

The door closed behind her. She stood on the granite steps, and looked up and down the street. Business men from the city were driving past, going home to their wives and children; they all looked comfortable and happy. In the west, a great bank of clouds was piled high, and still tinted red from the sunset. The lamps were lighted, and but few people were walking, and they were hurrying along homeward. Jennie yearned with an aching heart for the old farmhouse, for the two there who loved her beyond doubt or cavil, and she made up her mind quickly, to go back to them. Any home poverty could give was better than this homelessness, and her heart turned cold and hard to the woman upstairs.

"Yes," she thought to herself, "I will go to

the Winne's to-night; if they will not let me stay I will find Eva, and to-morrow I will send for my trunk and go home."

But many to-morrows came and went, and Jennie neither sent for her trunk nor went home!.

CHAPTER XVI.

TANGLED THREADS.

MARGARET HOLMES was very ill. The inmates of the Home walked about on tip-toe, and spoke in subdued whispers as they passed the sick girl's door. Many of them had not liked her particularly, and a few had shunned her; but now they all thought of her only as a helpless woman, fighting a cruel foe that was likely to worst her in the encounter. She had taken a deadly cold on that night when she went out to save Eva; she had forgotten to change the thin slippers she wore, and her feverish frame, already superinduced to illness, could no longer resist the aggressive power of disease. Her life had been so long one of denial and hardship, that it seemed useless to call together the remnant of its wasted forces to repel this last fierce invader. There seemed nothing to take hold of; no hope in the future of this life

"*She stood on the granite steps and looked up and down the street.*"—Page 142.

worth the effort to retain it. Worn and wasted by fever, without and within, Margaret no longer struggled or defied; she rested passive in the cruel yet kind arms, that were surely bearing her down to the banks of the dark river.

Eva was her faithful nurse and attendant, by night and day. She felt, in her remorse, that it would not be too much to give her own young life to save her friend, and no hand but hers was permitted to turn and cool the hot pillows, to pour out the bitter medicine, to bathe the feverish, wasting form. Eva's good, sensible mother had taught her, in her earliest years, a thorough knowledge of the care of the sick, and she turned it now to practical account. But it only eased the pain, it did not remove it.

Margaret grew worse, day by day, and at last sunk into a stupor which seemed to forebode death. The good, kind, old doctor, who saw such cases every day, and yet, strangely enough, did not become hardened — only philosophical — clasped his hands over his gold-headed cane, shook his head till the wide shirt-frill on his bosom trembled in sympathy, and looking at Eva said:

10

"You had better send for her friends, my dear."

"I — I believe she — has n't — any," replied Eva, between her sobs.

"So much the better, then; there will be fewer left to mourn. She may last this way several days; give the mixture when she needs a drink, and keep her quiet. Do n't cry, my dear; death is not the worst thing that can happen to us." He was retreating to the door, but came back. "Can I do anything further? Would a little money — "

"Thank you," answered Eva quietly; "we have enough." And the rather pompous, but really grand, old gentleman, of a past school, bowed himself out.

So Eva had nothing to do but watch and wait. She put the sick room in perfect order, wrote a little note home to her mother, saying she had left the store, and gave her reasons why, and then sat motionless for hours, listening to the fitful breathing, that sometimes almost stopped, and then grew loud and hard. Occasionally a low tap would summon her to the door, to answer an eager "how is she?" with a sorrowful shake of the head. Sometimes there would be given a glass of lemonade, or of cordial, for the sick girl, or a single hot-house flower, bought at a sacrifice of some small comfort.

Towards night of the third day Margaret Holmes stirred uneasily and at last opened her heavy eyes, with the light of recognition in them. She did not speak for a long time, but looked at every object in the room, and then at Eva, long and tenderly, with a gaze that was all-absorbing. Her eyes had grown large since her sickness, and now they seemed bright and dark. A color was stealing into her pale, sunken cheeks, and Eva wept with joy at the change.

"You are better, dear Margaret; you are going to get well. Oh, *how* glad I am to see you look like this."

Margaret smiled, ever so faintly. "Yes, I am better — I feel stronger — I shall soon be well. Eva dear, how long have I been sick?"

"Over two weeks. Oh, Margaret, you have been so ill; we were all worried about you, and now to think you are so much better — *it is too* good news. I must go and tell them all."

"Wait," said Margaret; "wait till to-morrow;

good news will keep. Now I want to see Mrs. Paine, and while she is here you must go out and take a long walk; but do not go near that store."

Eva protested that she did not need any fresh air, but Margaret held her point, through weakness that would not be denied. So Mrs. Paine, the kind matron of the Home, took Eva's place, while she went out to walk.

At first Eva did not know which way to turn. It was the day before Christmas, and a light fall of snow had frozen into a white, compact mass, over which the flying sleighs skimmed like birds. Eva followed them with her eyes, and noted the rosy cheeks and happy looks of the occupants, and heard the music of the jangling, snow-mad bells, and the laughter of hearts delirious with pleasure; but envied them not. It seemed as if she never could be unhappy again. She had escaped the foul disgrace of a tarnished name; her friend was given back to her from the dead. Eva was not a pious girl, in the common acceptation of that word, but she would have been little better than a heathen, if her heart had not gone out in gratitude to the protecting spirit of all good. She walked briskly on until she found herself on the gayest thoroughfare of the West Side, Washington street, and then she determined to go and call on Jennie Armstrong.

She had not seen Jennie since Thanksgiving, nor had she been at the Winne's. Margaret's severe illness had put every one else out of her mind; but she began to wonder that Jennie had not called to see her; Lucia had called one Sunday, but Eva, worn out with watching, was asleep and they would not disturb her. When she reached Mrs. Monroe's house and rang the bell, it was Sarah, the housemaid, who answered the call.

"Is Jennie—Miss Armstrong in?" asked Eva.

"No'm; she isn't here any more," answered Sarah; with a very expressive look on her bold face. Lower servants always dislike upper favorites.

"Not here? Why! when did she leave?"

"Nearly a month ago, Miss. The fact is, Miss"—lowering her voice to a rude whisper, "Missis turned her out of doors."

Eva stared at the girl in utter bewilderment. "Turned her out of doors! For what?"

"Do n't know, Miss; but she sent her off all in a minute, and we have never seen her since, and her trunk and all her things are here yet."

"I must see Mrs. Monroe," said Eva, making a motion to enter the house.

"I do n't think you can, Miss, if it's about her. But I'll take up your message, if you like."

"Tell her I'm a friend of Jennie Armstrong's and would like to have her address. I would like to see her and ask the question myself."

"I'm sure you can't see her, Miss, unless you was sent here from the Good Samaritans, or the Home for the Fallen, or the 'Dustrial School — that makes a difference; then you'd be a perishin' feller being, and she'd give you tracts, and let you work for your board. I'll go right up now, Miss."

The voluble Sarah soon returned, with a grin on her face.

"She do n't know nothin' about her; she do n't want to know nothin' about her. She plucked her like a brand a burnin', and now she's washed her hands of her forever. That's the message, word for word, Miss."

Eva was full of fiery indignation.

"I wish I could see that woman," she said; "I should just like to tell her what I think of her. I believe if Jennie Armstrong has gone wrong it is her doing." And she turned her back indignantly upon the closing door.

She turned her steps in the direction of Lucia's boarding place. Since Margaret's illness she had not seen much of Lucia; indeed, there had arisen a slight coolness between them, for Lucia disapproved of Margaret and the Home, both. She received Eva in her own room, however, pleasantly, if not cordially. She knew nothing of Jennie beyond the fact of her disappearance, of which she had recently heard.

"And you never looked after her to see what had become of her! Oh, Lucia, how could you?"

"I have nothing to do with it, Eva. I could not go about the streets looking after her. She knew what the consequences must be as well as any one. My brother thinks that she is somewhere in the city, under the protection of that Mr. Farnham, but he will not say anything about it; and he has forbidden my ever speaking to her again."

"Oh, Lucia, is n't it dreadful! He must have deceived her, for I am sure Jennie was always a good girl; she might have been a little thoughtless, but you know she was pure and innocent."

"Humph!" answered Lucia, coldly. "That does n't make her any better now. You know we warned her that evening at my brother's, but it seems it did no good, for she disappeared only a day or two after, and no one has seen her since."

"It will kill her mother," said Eva, wiping the tears away that were falling fast. "Have they heard about it in Newton?"

"Yes," replied Lucia; "but her parents do not believe it yet, and no one has the heart to tell them. They are waiting for Reuben Harlow to return, while he is lying between life and death at some hospital in the city, we could not find out where. That girl ought to suffer some of the misery she has caused."

"That girl! Why do you not rather say that man! If Jennie has gone wrong, and things do look rather against her, Ross Farnham is the one to blame. I believe now that Mrs. Monroe was acting as an agent for him, when she sent for

Jennie. Oh, Lucia! the trials and temptations for a girl in a city like this are just awful!"

"Nonsense," said Lucia, coldly. "If she behaves herself there is no more danger here than in her own home. Look at me! I do not meet with any temptations; I believe I am as presentable as other girls, but there are no plots and counterplots against me. It is vanity that causes all the trouble, Eva, vanity and frivolity. A girl with a high purpose in life and a mind above pleasures and amusements, will never come to any harm."

"Well," said Eva, slowly, "I am sorry for the butterflies, too; Jennie has seen so little of the bright side of life, that I expect she was blinded, poor girl! I wish we had looked after her closer. She needed old friends to protect her."

"Why did she need them any more than we do?" asked Lucia.

"You have your brother, and I—I have Margaret Holmes," answered Eva.

"I think you show questionable taste in the selection of your friends. There's Margaret Holmes, now; she is—"

"Hush!" said Eva, rising. "I cannot hear a

word against her, Lucia, and I must go right
back to her. And, oh, do send word to me if
you hear anything of Jennie. I am going home
as soon as Margaret recovers; the city stifles me,
and all I earn is eaten up by expenses, so that at
the end of a year I should be no better off finan-
cially than if I had staid in Newton. I would
rather have only two calico dresses a year there,
than silks and velvets here."

"What a strange girl!" said Lucia to herself,
as Eva closed the hall door after her and she
went back to her own cosy room, "I cannot
understand why those girls have so much trouble.
I don't believe it is true that shop-girls have
peculiar trials. And Jennie was not a shop-girl,
but had every chance to improve and cultivate
her mind. How could she be so infatuated as to
believe in that Ross Farnham! Yes, she must
have been naturally bad!"

With these thoughts, Lucia dismissed the
subject and turned her attention to the discovery
of what Philip II. did with himself after his
wife's death.

Calm, passionless, ruled by her head and not
by her heart, with an intense self-esteem, that

never could be tempted to lower itself, how could Lucia Winne appreciate the sensitive weakness, the tender, loving, trusting nature of another woman? *She* did not crave love. At some time, probably, a proper offer would be made her, by some one she could highly esteem and respect, and after she should be married decorously, there would be time enough for sentiment, if, indeed, any such weakness was necessary. Such women are invaluable to the world. In life and in death they are eulogized; their calm, philosophical natures create no trouble, and accept none. But to the wayward, tortured, restless soul of the average sinner, they are about as soothing and comfortable as rocks of adamant.

CHAPTER XVII.

MARGARET'S STORY.

"Beyond the smiling and the weeping."

HEN Eva left Lucia she walked rapidly toward the Home, aware that she had been absent longer than she had intended, and anxious lest Margaret should need her. She hurried on until she reached the door, when she saw the Matron of the Home looking for her, with eyes wet with tears.

"Oh, is she worse? Will she die?" asked Eva, wildly.

"I am afraid she will," replied the kind-hearted little woman, with whom Margaret had always been a favorite. "Perhaps that is n't the worst thing that could happen to her; but it does seem so dreadful to die, away from home and friends and among strangers. I believe she is an orphan, but there must be somebody belonging to her."

Eva hurried into the house, greatly alarmed. She had not thought for a moment that Margaret would die. The sick girl was raised on pillows, and the curtain was drawn away from the west window, that she might look on the sunset, the golden light of which flooded the room, the bed, and the recumbent figure with a splendor of rose and gold. A small table with writing apparatus stood by the bed. Margaret looked better and stronger; Eva could see no cause for fresh alarm. She put her things away and took up her post of nurse again, feeling physically invigorated by her walk, but mentally depressed by the strange news of Jennie. She did not intend to tell Margaret, but the sick girl saw that something had occurred, and Eva told her all.

It did not surprise her as it had Eva; she knew Mrs. Monroe and her kind, and was prepared for such a climax. When Eva had gone down to her tea and returned, Margaret said, in her own natural voice, stronger and clearer than it had been yet:

"I feel like talking to-night, Eva. Lock the door so that we shall not be disturbed; now, wheel the lounge up to the side of the bed, and put on your wrapper. You can lie and rest while we talk. I am going to tell you my own story.

"I was born in Belleville, a little town in Maine; my father was the practicing physician of the place, and he made a comfortable fortune, enough to keep us all respectably. My own mother was dead, but I could not remember her, and my step-mother, a good, kind, judicious woman, filled her place admirably. I never could understand the prejudice against step-mothers; mine was the best and truest friend I ever had, and when she died I mourned her as though she had been mine by nature instead of adoption.

"In one year I lost her, my father, and every dollar in the world; the last was the result of an endorsement. My elder and only brother, a boy of good impulses and kind heart, but easily led by others, had got into a wild way of living, and in some manner became involved in a disgraceful bank robbery. His share of the matter being discovered, my father endorsed his note for the amount; the note was never paid, and my father sacrificed every dollar to meet the demand. He died shortly after, of a malignant fever, and the mother soon followed him. It was seven or eight years ago that it all happened.

"I was then eighteen years old, without a relative in this country; my father was English, and our kindred were all beyond the sea. I came with a family to Chicago, because I was acquainted with them, and I wanted to get away from those who knew of our fallen fortunes. My brother, Horace, I have never heard·from, but presume he went to England; if he ever visited Belleville, he could have found no clue to my whereabouts, for I was angry and could not tolerate his memory, much as we had loved each other in childhood. Ah, if the great God should deal with us as we deal with fellow sinners, it will go hard with many of us at the closing account! There were circumstances in the poor boy's life I did not take into consideration. My father was wrapped up in his profession; my brother had been influenced by injudicious friends to dislike our step-mother, and rebel against her authority; I was at school, and he ran away from home with two other boys, the scapegrace sons of rich fathers, when only seventeen years

old.   My father felt his disgrace keenly, and
would not expostulate with the recreant boy, or
try to win him back; and his bank exploit was
the last we ever heard of him.   But now I must
tell you about myself.   Give me one spoonful
from that tumbler, my lips are so dry.

"Child, I have often wondered why God made
one set of people black and another white; one
weak and another strong!   Perhaps I shall know
soon, but I am not sure that the knowledge will
compensate for a wasted life.   I began fair
enough; perhaps I was too strong in my own
strength.   I worked hard for meagre wages, and
kept my honesty and integrity, but demanded
that the world should appreciate both.   The world
just rolled its chariot wheels over me.   A few
good people held out dry theological husks for
my moral digestion, but society ignored me; I
had culture, but not wealth.   I craved pleasure,
not sinful pleasure, but just the gladsome side
of life.   Well — it must be told — my employer
offered me all; not in so many words; not by any
base contract; but by little acts of attention and
kindness, and by making my work less; by drawing me gradually into the social charm of his

own atmosphere; by cruel and false sophistries. I was too blind and vain to read the truth. A few months I was his favorite, and was envied, hated, and shunned by the people among whom I moved. Oblivious to taunts and jeers, I spent my days in the store, for appearance sake, but my nights were devoted to pleasure seeking and such amusements as are free to the public.

"Then came an awakening that rent soul and body. Months of shame, and darkness, and anguish ensued, but my soul came out of the flame purified. I repented in dust and ashes. I left all my old associations and stood, clothed and in my right mind, on the threshold of a new life. Every door was then shut in my face except that of the Magdalen Asylum. I went back to the man who had ruined my life — the man from whom I have saved you — and I demanded of him the only compensation he could give me, the right to earn my honest bread at his hands. I think I frightened him; he gave me the place with the same pay that any other clerk would have for the same work. It was part of my punishment to stand there and endure the sneers

11

of those who knew me; to see the hideousness of my sin as they saw it.

"Child, when you came something drew me to you. Oh, how glad I am that I have been permitted to watch over you. I have told you my story as a warning. Be thankful for the dry bread of an honest life, for the homeliest, narrowest path in which ever woman walked, for the garb that will make you a fright in its plainness, rather than for the purple and fine linen for which you must sell your birthright. Eva, darling, you will not love me less, now that you know what my life has been, now that you understand the manifold temptations that crowd the life of a young and thoughtless girl, who must cope, single-handed, with the Devil of Sensuality?"

Margaret Holmes lay back exhausted on her pillow, and Eva dropped the invigorating cordial between her pale lips, till life and strength seemed again to return. Very lovingly, too, she kissed her, uttering sweet, soothing words of hope and encouragement. Margaret smiled faintly, and drew Eva's fair head down on the pillow.

" How long, how dark the way has been! But it seems lighter now; where I failed once I might fail again. Eva, are you warm, are you quite easy, dear?"

" Quite. And oh, so happy, Margaret, because you are better. You will soon be well again."

" Yes," said Margaret; " very, very soon. And now, dear child, try to sleep."

It did not need much trying on Eva's part. The weight of anxiety was lifted from her heart, and she fell asleep in Margaret's arms. The older woman did not sleep so soon; the night-lamp, burning low, cast fantastic shadows about the room, and it seemed to her excited fancy that they took upon them a weird resemblance to undefined forms, that came near and looked at her and wrung their shadowy hands. And then the light dropped lower, and the pale, yellow moonlight filled the room, and Margaret's soul was filled with a strange, ineffable peace and sweetness. Her weary eyes closed on all the dim outlines, the weird and shifting shadows, the vexing, perplexing mysteries of life, and with her head bowed upon Eva's, she, too, slept.

It was broad daylight when Eva felt herself

shaken, and aroused from sweet sleep and pleasant dreams. The Matron was bending over her, crying. She turned quickly and looked at Margaret; her face was white and peaceful. She was still sleeping!

CHAPTER XVIII.

OVER!

"Foolish! most women are that, you know.
Fond and foolish; God makes them so."

WHEN Jennie Armstrong left Mrs. Monroe's inhospitable roof she was in a half unconscious state of mind, so overwhelmed was she by her sudden and unexpected discharge. What had she done, or failed to do, that had aroused Mrs. Monroe's wrath in such a violent manner? She walked along the streets like one in a dream, and it was all she could do to keep from a violent and childlike fit of crying. She turned in the direction of the Winne's, determined she would ask them to receive her for this night only, and in the morning she would go back to her home; back to poverty and obscurity.. It was, at least, better than this homelessness. All the faces that looked at her swam

(165)

through a sea of tears. A stronger nature
would have been nerved to bravery and independence by such injustice, but she was as helpless
in these wide, noisy streets as any child. She
was not even sure that she knew the way to Mr.
Winne's; the houses loomed up like giants, in
the twilight, and the streets seemed to wander
and mix themselves up inextricably. A tear fell
and rested on her little cold hands; another and
another followed. She could not see her way
now for the hot, blinding shower; she stumbled
at a stone coping and would have fallen, had not
some one caught her. An arm was extended,
awkwardly but surely, and a cheery voice cried:

"Why, you poor child! out alone at this time
of day, or night, rather, and crying, too? Why,
what has happened, you poor, forlorn, little girl!
Are you lost in the streets?" Then, as both her
little cold hands were gathered into his warm
ones, the rescuer murmured: "Jennie, darling,
what is it?"

The arch hypocrite! how dared he!

Jennie gave one look, to assure herself that it
was indeed Ross Farnham, and then she threw
herself, recklessly, foolishly, but oh, so blissfully,

into his arms, and fell into convulsions of crying.

"My darling! my darling!" he whispered the words over and over to her, and then told her, soothingly, that his carriage was near. He had seen her in passing, and knew the forlorn, drooping figure; and he would take her wherever she wanted to go, only, first, she must accompany him and have a warm, comfortable supper, and tell him all about her trouble, and how it had happened.

Now, why did not her mother's God send one of His ministering angels to save her; to whisper one word of warning, to rescue this innocent soul from the tempter's power, to show her how dark and deep and awful was that chasm on whose flower-wreathed brink she stood? Answer me, theologians, who reason that

> "With Adam's fall
> We sinned all."

Why did the tempter prevail?

Her mother was praying for her; her poor mother, who had sacrificed so much in parting from her! This girl's soul was, of itself, pure and stainless; she had no conception of sin, as yet; she was going to her doom with the blind faith and trust of a loving child, as thousands of innocent girls have gone before her, as thousands of innocent girls will follow! And yet, the Christian says, God lives!

He does! Stronger than sin, He shall ultimately rescue every soul from its bondage; infinite in existence, He shall draw all essence of being to Him, and in that gracious Presence it shall grow and live forever and ever.

I do not know why I stopped to say this, unless the theme inspired me. I dislike moral sandwiches; they are not always palatable.

Jennie followed Ross Farnham very willingly, and it needs no brilliant imagination to realize the transition from the cold, shivering, lonesome streets at nightfall, to the warm, comfortable, lighted carriage, that would speedily bear them to cheeriness and safety. They drove to a popular and fashionable restaurant, and were soon seated in a luxurious room, at a table spread with a delicious supper. "The anchorite may turn up his holy nose at creature comforts, but I never yet saw a famished sinner that could not be brought to his knees quicker by a hot meal, or a smoking draught, than by any amount of tracts

and bibles peddled out by the spiritual-minded
agent of salvation. Jennie's spirits rose with
the warmth and food; she had eaten nothing that
day. The red came into her cheeks, and she
recovered her old, gay, *insouciant* manner.

Ross Farnham had been watching her with
that tender solicitude, which almost any man
can assume at will toward almost any woman,
always excepting those who have a right to it.
For the time being he loved, idolized, worshiped
her, and would have killed any man who dared
to dispute it. Looking at her, and thinking this,
he touched the bell.

" Champagne," he said to the waiter; "a quart
bottle." And he named a favorite brand.

Jennie stopped him peremptorily. " No, no,"
she said; " I must not drink wine; it would not
be right. Indeed, indeed, it would not."

" Little innocent!" laughed Ross. " Champagne is not wine; it is nothing more than cider.
Why, you could drink it like water, and it would
never hurt you. See here, you shall fill your
glass with raisins and watch them bead and
sparkle and plunge in a sea of diamonds. There
is no harm in it, darling. You can trust me."

And no fire came down from Heaven to consume him!

Jennie resisted bravely. She belonged to a family that believed in moderate drinking, and unfortunately had not instilled that horror of intoxicating liquors that is a principle in itself. She had never tasted wine, and it seemed an unwomanly thing to do.

"Oh, Ross, drink it for me; indeed, I cannot bear to taste it. Let me play with mine. What a lovely, lovely color! Amber, isn't it? How pure and sparkling!"

"Jennie," said Ross Farnham, in his dangerously seductive tones. "Do you love me, darling?"

"God knows I do," answered the girl, with unwonted earnestness. The smile faded from her face, and great tears stood in her loving eyes.

"Do you love me better than any one in the world?"

"Better! Yes! oh, yes!"

"Better than father or mother, friends or kindred?"

"Yes, Ross; I do."

"Say it after me, better than father or mother, friends or kindred."

And she repeated the sentence, word for word.

"And now, darling," taking her wine-glass in his hand, "if you love me, pledge me with this; you will prove your loyalty, my own."

It was done! She lifted the golden liquid and touched it to the tender chrism of her lips, and then set the empty glass on the table before her.

Ross Farnham took a shining diamond circlet from his vest pocket, and slipped it on the dainty white forefinger, guarding it there with a plain, heavy, gold band.

"Mine!" he whispered, fondly, gathering the girl in his arms.

CHAPTER XIX.

THE RETURN HOME.

"The deep damnation of his taking off."

THE train upon which Eva Bartlett was returning to her home in Newton, stopped within a station of that place, for dinner. She was weary and lonely, and gladly left the close cars for the hurried meal. She had changed somewhat in appearance, was thinner and paler, the result of watching by the sick-bed of her friend. It was for Margaret, Eva wore such deep black, purchased out of respect to her memory, and from real, true affection, not simply because she inherited her friend's savings.

She returned to the car, feeling rested and refreshed by the change; as she stood on the platform she noticed a feeble looking man, who gazed about him as if uncertain of his surroundings. Something in his appearance struck her

as being familiar, and as he turned and looked
at her she recognized him fully, and started in
dismay. It was Jennie Armstrong's father.
Always retiring and unsocial in his manner, he
had never been a favorite with the young people,
or noticed them much, but now, as he saw and
recognized Eva, he sprang eagerly toward her,
and his air of dejection gave way to one of eager
enquiry.

Eva's first thought was to evade him, and pass
into the car as if unconscious of his presence;
but he was too intent on his own purpose to
notice this, and following her, with a quick,
nervous movement, he laid a thin, cold hand on
her shoulder just as she reached her seat. She
turned, and saw a white, worn face, aged and
wrinkled by despair, and sealed with the sign
manual of death, yet from which a longing hope
seemed to flash the intelligence of a soul's
anguish. Eva shook hands with the poor father,
with her eyes averted that he might not see the
tears in them. He was the first to speak; she
could not.

"So you have come back again?" he said, with
a vacant attempt to smile that was pitiful to see.

"And now, tell me "— his voice sank to a fierce whisper, and he grasped her arm till she writhed with the pain —" where is Jennie?"

To have saved her life, at that moment Eva could not have spoken a word, neither could she look at the miserable father; she kept her eyes fixed upon the car window, that looked wet and blurred as in a rain storm, and yet the sun shone.

"Where is Jennie?" he repeated earnestly. "You must know something about her. Is she dead?"

"Yes!" Eva was driven now to desperation. "Yes, Mr. Armstrong, she is dead; dead to you and to all of us who loved her!" And she covered her face with her hands, and wept.

"Oh, my God! then it is true, it is true," groaned the heart-broken man. "May my bitterest curse —"

"Hush!" Eva laid her hand upon his lips. "Do not curse your child, Mr. Armstrong. Try and think the best of her that you can; we all believe that it was the cruelest treachery that betrayed her into that man's hands. She must have a place in your heart, when —"

"You do not know what you are talking

about," interrupted Mr. Armstrong, harshly. "It will kill her mother; she has added the vilest disgrace to our poverty; we have, at least, been respectable, but we can never hold our heads up again. Oh, if we could have buried her in decency and honor, though in a pine coffin and a Potter's field, it would have been happiness."

The father broke out into the fiercest invectives against the destroyer of his child, and Eva sat frightened and silent, until the cars reached Newton, and she saw her mother and the children waiting for her. At another time she would have felt some consequence from the change in her circumstances, perhaps, and realized that she was now able to maintain her family in comfort, but all thoughts of herself were merged in sympathy for those unhappy parents. As she stepped on the platform, a sad, white face caught her attention; to avoid those wistful, agonized eyes she turned quickly away and drew her mother and the delighted children one side.

"It is Mrs. Armstrong," she whispered to her mother; "I would not see her for the world. Is n't it awful, that look on her face?"

"She would not see you," replied her mother.

"She has not spoken to any one since the news came. Mr. Armstrong went up to meet you first, Eva. Is it true?"

"Yes! but do not talk of it here, before the children. I can hardly believe it myself. Oh, mother, I could have told him of her death so much easier."

Mr. Armstrong met his wife and drew her arm through his.

"Did you walk down, Mary?" he asked, in a steady voice.

"Yes, Richard. This is not all you have to say; where is Jennie? Where is our child?"

"Never speak her name to me again, Mary. We have no child! our children are in Heaven. She — oh, God! it cannot be true." And the man shook with the agony of the thought.

His wife looked up into his face. All light of intelligence had died out of hers.

"Richard," she asked presently, in a low voice, "is it true; is Jennie lost?"

"Yes, it is true! all true! Did I not say you should never mention her name? May the curses of — "

"Hush, Richard! You must not curse our

child. Dear little thing! do you remember how sweet and pretty she was? Yes, yes; I will find her again; she is not lost to her mother."

They walked the rest of the way home in silence. At the house door Mr. Armstrong left his wife to grope her way in alone; it was not dark, but she walked like a dreaming person, and looking after her, he saw her stagger as she entered the door. Such a look as came over his face then, as it paled with the white heat of a man's despair; all the weakness and uncertainty of his life seemed lifted from him in that moment.

He went into the rickety old barn, and pulled the door together after him. Above the window on two rests, hung an old gun, a true shooter, as he knew, for it had brought down many a dinner for them. As he lifted his hand to take it down his eye fell on a little, dust-covered book, lying on the top of the low window. He took it and looked at it a moment, with white, compressed lips; then he opened it, and saw *her* name. With a sullen, smothered oath, he hurled it from him, and as it struck the floor with a dull thud, he muttered fiercely:

12

"False to her mother — false to herself — false to God! I have lived too long; let this end it."

A moment later there was a loud report.

Oh, coward! who could leave a weak woman to bear a double burden of grief and shame, while you slept in a dastard's grave! Was it from you the daughter inherited the weakness of loving too well? Was it the sin of the father visited upon the child?

CHAPTER XX.

REAPING THE REWARD.

"Only — O God! O God! to cry for bread
And get a stone! Daily to lay my head
Upon a bosom where the old love 's dead."

T was a beautiful Spring day, and the streets of Chicago were crowded with a throng of people — men, intent on business; women, intent on pleasure; with an undercurrent of struggling humanity of either sex. The stores were gay with Spring goods, and the fashionable resorts were surrounded by elegant carriages, from which well-dressed ladies descended, comfortably and luxuriously, by the aid of sleek coachmen.

It was matinee day at the theatres; at the prominent one they were playing "Camille," and a popular star had attracted all classes thither. The house was crowded; virtue and vice outbid each other. Even the boxes, those *bete noirs* of theatrical managers, were all taken. In one of those boxes sat a young and beautiful woman, who, dressed in the height of elegant fashion, was the attraction of all eyes; she looked like a queen of society, except that she was alone and unattended. She had occupied that same box a number of times lately, and the elegance of her costume had not failed to arouse the admiration and envy of every woman who saw it. She was never overdressed; there was not the slightest shade of over-color, not a flower or ribbon too many; her dress was a combination of silk and velvet, exquisitely fitting her slender form. The hand that held the gold and pearl lorgnette was faultlessly gloved; the one that lay idly in her lap revealed a diamond that shone like a star.

It was not alone her elegant toilette that drew attention to her, but her subtle, fascinating beauty, which was heightened, not marred, by the shadow of pensiveness. It was a fresh-tinted, girlish beauty, without any hard lines; there was enough of character to reveal a thinking soul beneath, and a charming air of culture and refinement to redeem it from mere prettiness.

Over it all rested a shade of melancholy; the dark eyes had a wistful, weary, troubled look, and the delicate, rosebud mouth was drooping and sorrowful!

Mrs. Ross Farnham! Called so from courtesy by the men of his set, and scorned and spurned by the women! As pure in heart as any young wife, yet an object of contempt to the man who had perilled his soul to ruin her, and who had wearied of her in a few short months.

Yes, Jennie was hovering on the border land of sin. It was very pleasant at first, when she was living in the rapture of a first love, with conscience, remorse, memory, all stifled in the rose-colored atmosphere, drowned in costly draughts of pleasure. There was no time to think, no way to escape while love stood sentinel at the door. For a while the world seemed well lost to Jennie?

She had not heard from either father or mother as yet; she was not surprised that they had cast her off, when at times she fully realized what she had done. She had written a few hasty, penitent words, and Ross had taken them to the post office; but they were never answered.

How could they be, when they were never received?

Then she had sought out the hospital where Reuben Harlow still languished from his wound; but he would not see her. He was too ill, the nurses said, when her name was taken in. She sent him some rare flowers, and in the centre of the basket hid a tiny note, begging piteously for some word of her dear mother. The sick man was asleep when the flowers came; his old mother watched beside him, holding the flowers on her lap against the time of his awaking. When he roused from the short sleep in which he found occasional brief rest from the pain of his wounded lungs, he murmured a name faintly:

"Jennie! Jennie, darling! Is it you?"

Then he awoke fully and saw the flowers.

"Take them away," he said, sternly; "throw them in the street! I thought I was home again, and she was there, with her wicked beauty and her soft smiles, and her fondness, betraying and deceiving! But what am I saying? She could not help it, poor child; fate was against her. But throw the flowers away, mother; they would kill me!"

So her pleading little appeal was cast aside, unnoticed, and hearing no word from it, she thought, sadly, " Reuben hates me, and no wonder!"

But it had not mattered so much then; she had Ross' love, and was not that compensation enough for putting her soul in peril and losing all her friends?

Jennie gave the great world no chance to snub her with its jeers and frowns; she walked alone. Once she met Mr. Winne and Lucia face to face; she was so glad to see one from the old life that she stopped before she thought. Could she ever forget with what scorn Mr. Winne drew his sister away! How thankful she was that they could not see the hot blood dye her cheeks and forehead after they had passed, and then she had swept on, velvet-dressed, lace-crowned, and beautiful, a target for the impertinent admiration of men and the gratuitous insolence of women.

Was she happy? No, no; a thousand times, no! She was walking a delirious measure to the strains of enchanted music; her senses were captivated and conscience slept. It needed but a touch to arouse her, and a single tear of contrition would forever dissolve her pearl of love.

She was conscious, on this day at the theatre, of living in a world alone. Helen Stearns, the woman in whose care Ross had placed her, had no reason to like her, and there was nothing in common between them. With those like herself she would not associate; with the respectable and virtuous she could not. Somehow, she was weary of it all. She had sold herself for love, and only golden fetters remained. She clasped her hands desperately above the gold and pearl opera-glass, and looked about the house.

Fashionable young men — rich loafers — had dropped in to note who was present, and leaned, kid-gloved and moustached, about the doors, commenting rudely upon the beauty of "Mrs. Farnham," as they superciliously styled her. She could not hear them, but she noted the glances they exchanged, and felt more than ever her isolated position. Why was not Ross there to protect her, for at least there was protection from insult in his presence; and then she recalled the fact that he was seldom with her in those days. The inevitable end was coming, and this was the beginning of the end.

She turned her attention to the play, but it was not diverting; the stage Camille was apostrophizing the children from the window, to which, in mortal weariness and weakness, she had dragged herself. It was the most touching scene in the drama. Jennie feared she should cry, and would not listen; so, while all were intensely regarding the stage Magdalen, the real one, gathered up her luxurious wrappings, and passed out. It was only a few paces to her carriage; the coachman held the door open with the utmost respect, and Jennie, placing one dainty foot upon the step, was about to enter, when a hand, light as a snow-flake, fell upon her shoulder.

She turned hastily, with something of a nervous shiver, and an uncanny tremor ran through her frame, as though a spirit in passing had touched her! Pshaw! there was nothing to be frightened at —'only an old beggar woman, ragged and bent, who peered into her face with eager persistence. Yet it was not an ordinary beggar, for she did not ask alms; she only smiled and muttered, and shook her head. When Jennie turned at her touch, the woman scanned each feature closely, passed her thin hands over the velvet of her dress, and asked in a weird whisper:

"Have you seen Jennie? She is lost!"

The coachman thrust her away and helped his mistress into her carriage, where she sank unconscious on the cushions. She had stood face to face with her mother!

CHAPTER XXI.

LOST AND FOUND.

SHE was only a poor old woman, sick, weak, and crazed ; the boys jeered at her on the street, and walked in rough and ragged procession after her. Occasionally, when out of sight of a policeman, they threw sticks and stones at her, which wounded the poor old creature's limbs and brought tears into her weak, faded eyes; but she never resisted them or made a complaint, she only walked on and on wearily, always in a circle of streets. She passed by men and boys with compressed, close-shut lips, but every young girl she met she would try to stop, and would cling to her, and beseech her, in such a pitiful tone:

"Have you seen my child? Have you seen Jennie? Oh, you must have seen her! Let me tell you how she looks. She's so pretty; oh, such lovely dimples, and a face like a baby's;

and oh! the smallest, prettiest hands, and such a gay, happy smile. I tell you, you must have seen her; she's lost! Do you hear? I must find her — I must take her home to her father— he's waiting for her. She's lost, but I'm her mother — I'll find her. Ah, dear lady, help me to find her. I tell you she is lost! lost! lost!"

Her voice, as she went on, would gradually rise to a shriek, and she would beat the air with her pale hands, and then the grim guardians of the peace would drag her away and lock her up in a cell of the station house, where she would stretch her thin hands through the iron gratings, and chant the same weird story to every passer-by, till the officials wearied of her, and finding her friendless and penniless, turned her out again.

She was worn, almost as thin as a shadow; her scant gray hair floated over her shoulders like spectral fantasies of fashion, and her few ragged clothes were pathetic in their appeal for sympathy. As she walked she constantly muttered and shook her head, and moaned to herself. She had traveled many miles that weary day, following some false clue of her crazed brain, when she laid her hand on the shoulder of the beautiful

woman stepping into the carriage in front of the
pretty theatre; as the lady hurried away and left
her, she turned, not more disappointed than
usual, but with some new feeling, that was not
cold, nor hunger, nor disappointment, but was a
strange and painful perplexity. She dwelt upon
that meeting, upon that beautiful, horror-stricken
face, which only flashed upon her's for a moment,
and she walked on until exhausted, and then sat
down on the steps of a clothing store. The proprietor, a dark, heavy-browed man, came out and
spurned her with his foot; she rose meekly, and
wandered off until she came to a street where
there were dwellings; at the basement of one she
stopped and asked for something to eat; the boy
who opened the door set the dog upon her! But
at the next house a good, kindly Irish girl —
God bless her! — took her into the kitchen, and
set her down to a warm supper.

"Poor innocent," said the kind girl; "shure
it's starved, and cold, and wretched intirely, ye
are, and the wits wanting, too! Holy Mother
presarve ye! It's a hard world for the like of
yees!"

The supper gave her strength to move on, and

she wandered back again into the dense heart of the city, until she found herself at the beautiful theatre once more. It was all sparkle and light; all glitter! glitter! Handsome carriages rolled up to the door, and splendidly dressed ladies got out, all silk and lace and diamonds, with sweet smiles and dainty manner! She watched for the lady in the purple velvet, the lovely lady with the great dark eyes; but the pompous coachmen ordered her rudely out of the way, and threatened her with their whips.

She became confused and frightened; the lamps turned into a sea of fire; and then — and then, somebody touched her — somebody wound tender, loving arms about her, and as the cold night air seemed to creep about her lips and cheeks with a caress, and the stars came down to meet the city lights, and all was a drear chaos of voices and lights and far-off music — then, oh, then, somebody received her falling weight in the closest, lovingest embrace, and clinging arms were thrown fondly about her.

It was only a girl, in a coarse dress and a red shawl; but she had found Jennie! Mother and child had met at last.

CHAPTER XXII.

THE NARROW PATH.

"Said I not so? that I would sin no more!
Witness, my God, I did;
Yet I am run again upon the score:
My faults cannot be hid."

 YEAR of harrowing experiences had passed — what need to tell of them — since Jennie had given up all sinful luxuries, and left a few farewell words for Ross Farnham, that I think he will remember in his dying hour. She had not looked upon his face; she heard the story of doom, and saw herself as she really was in the eyes of the world.

Oh, such a bitter, hand-to-hand fight with poverty; such a rending, snarling, gnawing wolf at the door to bait with flesh and blood, and no ravens to come, as they did to Elijah. Through it all, too, there was a sad, desolate, dying mother, mercifully insensible to mere bodily discomfort, but haunted by spectres of the past; daily, hourly, wringing her daughter's heart by allusions to her wrong-doing.

Oh, what need of a future place of punishment! Is there any boiling caldron, where the fire is hotter than the white heat of remorse? I think Jennie walked into frequent pits of red sulphur at this period of her life. These were, her dying mother, brought to this terrible pass by her daughter's weakness, and her dead father. Night and day he stood before her, stern, vindictive, unforgiving. No need of a jury to convict her, or of a frowning judge to read her sentence. Her only merit was that she wore her crown of thorns worthily. There was no crying over the life she had relinquished, with its ease and luxury; she accepted all the hardships of her lot as steps upward, and toiled, day after day, at whatever she could find to do, until health and strength both failed her. She could not leave her sick mother, so her work must be taken home, whatever it might be. It seemed at this time that if only one of her old friends would come to her rescue, it would be like a hand extended from Heaven.

One day she was returning home from a useless search after work, in a most despondent mood. I call home the miserable refuge which she shared with her mother, and in the sense of refuge it was a home. She was nearer a condition of recklessness to-day than she had yet been since she set out in this new, narrow path, for every door seemed shut against her, shut and barred. Ross Farnham had offered, through his lawyer, to assist her, but she would neither see him nor hear from him. She had left her jewels, even to the ring with which he foreswore himself, and her costly wardrobe, with every other token of the brief idolatry of his love, and had carried away with her only the simple serge dress and coarse shawl she had worn when Ross met and deceived her.

Upon this day she had just left a beautiful house where lived a lady who had promised her work a week previous. When Jennie called for it, however, the lady informed her that she had felt it incumbent upon her, as a church member, to give it to a young girl who had an invalid father to support; besides — and this was evidently the whole turning-point — *she* would do

13

it at half price. There was no more to be said; the obligations of poverty at half price were not to be gainsaid; but Jennie wondered how much longer body and soul could be kept together.

Was it surprising, then, that she was quite disheartened? She had eaten no food since the morning, and she was weary in flesh and spirit. Oh, dear Savior, who wast tempted and lonely, dost Thou see Thy children at such times, and know how pitiful is their fate?

As she walked along, with downcast eyes, she nearly ran over a little mother, who was trundling a perambulator along, with one baby in it, while another toddled at her side. Jennie lifted her eyes and began an apology, and then suddenly stopped short — it was Mrs. Winne! She almost smiled in her cold despair, on seeing the nervous haste with which the woman drew her skirts aside and gathered her little brood about her, as though violent hands were about to be laid on them. Then for a moment the two stood and looked at each other — the woman who had home, husband, children, and an honest name, and the woman who had lost all. Heavens! how souls, lost or saved, can look out of human eyes!

Jennie could not help appealing to her at that supreme moment of her misery; but at the first intimation of speech, Mrs. Winne seemed to pale and shrink in extreme displeasure and surprise, and then she trundled her offspring away, and hurried home to tell Albert of the shameless audacity of that miserable girl!

The blow struck home. I will not deny that Jennie hated Mrs. Winne fiercely at that moment, and wished she could recall her to tell her so. Then she tried to forget her utterly, and accept this penance as another offering to the Moloch of her fate.

When she reached the shabby entrance that led to her poor retreat, something rose up before her and she started back, appalled. What was it— ghost or spirit? She gave a quick involuntary cry of convulsive fear, as she saw the wreck of Reuben Harlow! Her first thought was that he would kill her, and she bowed her head, not daring to look up, until his voice re-assured her. There was no attempt at greeting.

"I have seen your mother," he said, calmly; "and she knew me."

"Oh, Reuben!" cried Jennie, in distress;

"why did you come here? I heard that you were — you were — " She hesitated.

" Dying? Well, yes, I am; but I am a long time about it. Sometimes I think I must have a dozen lives, I hang on so. Well, I could n't save you, Jennie; I tried, but fate was against me. Still, I felt that you might need me, and I came as soon as they would let me; and I am so glad I did."

Glad! Jennie wondered what he could be glad about. She was fast losing her beauty — sorrow and suffering do not perpetuate the bloom of youth — and as to his love; oh, surely that must be dead now. She waited.

" I am glad," he continued, coughing feebly at intervals, " to know that you are safe. Oh, Jennie, child, was it worth while to gain the whole world and lose your own soul! You do not think so, or you would not be here. Oh, thank God, that I find you in honest rags rather than in the purple and fine linen of sin! Oh, if my hand had not failed; if his perfidious soul had — "

" Hush! Reuben," said Jennie, solemnly, with a far-away look in her dark, sad eyes. " I loved him — that is all my excuse — I loved him from the first moment I saw him; my sin has brought its punishment. Do you remember how plump my cheeks and arms were? Now I am nearly as thin as you. Oh, Reuben, do you think I have not suffered since I came to my senses, as I thought of you, lying a whole year and more in that dreary hospital on my account! How can I live with such a load of guilt on my soul!"

"It is not your guilt; it is his! Can you not see the arch hypocrite's whole plan? It was to place you in his power that his cousin sent for you; it was to help his designs that she turned you into the streets. You see I know it all. Why, poor little lamb, you had not the shadow of a chance!"

" I did not intend to be wicked, Reuben," said Jennie, in a low tone. "I did not realize my danger until it was too late. Try not to think of me as a bold, bad girl; I can see now that I was led astray by those whom I trusted the most."

" And he — the villain who caused it all. Jennie, I swore a thousand times that I would kill him if I got well; but I am a dying man myself.

I must forego my revenge, or leave it to Him, who has said, 'Vengeance is mine, I will repay.' Oh, he will be punished, never fear! Have you seen him since — since you left him?"

"No," answered Jennie, wearily; her strength was fast failing her. "That is, not to speak to him. But, Reuben, let us not talk of him; I cannot bear it. I will only tell you this, I loved him better than my own soul; I love him now. My heart breaks with loneliness when I think of him; you see I am not cured. Bad as I am, and unfit to be the associate of good people, who are Christians, in the sight of God I am his wife, and I shall be at the judgment day."

Reuben Harlow groaned. Just so he loved her, and to what had it brought him? To ruin, desolation, and death! And yet he was as nothing in her sight. He held out his hand in farewell, but she did not offer to take it.

"Good-bye," he said hoarsely; "I have only a little while to live; let me help you if you need me. I am going back to the old place. Promise me, Jennie, by the memory of the years when we were so happy together, that you will send to me, if you want me while I live; but if — if I must go soon — oh, God, how can I say good-bye forever! "

" Not forever, Reuben; and indeed, I would ask you first, of all the world, to befriend me. Good-bye, and God bless you, Reuben ; if He will hear me."

And Reuben walked feebly away, coughing and tottering like an old man. Jennie looked after him, and hot tears of anguish rolled down her cheeks. The night had darkened and the stars were shining faintly in the blue sky, far, far above her. There was only a small square of Heaven visible, but how calm and peaceful it looked! How often she had watched those same stars from the old farm-house, and mused upon the beautiful, far-off world she longed to see and know. And how had it served her?

Tears blotted out the stars and the heavens, and she went into the house, and groped her way to the two poor rooms she and her mother occupied.

CHAPTER XXIII.

THE GOSPEL OF PEACE.

"Not God had wrought her hapless woe,
   Had sent her wandering to and fro.
   She did not fear, alone with Him,
   Though sense were dead, and soul were dim.
   From man the blow that killed her came,
   From man her craving grief and shame,
   On him lay all the bitter blame,
      From him she asked her child."

Y E 'D better rouse yourself, Miss. It 's them undertaker's men a coming."

They were bringing in a pine coffin, with much unnecessary noise and shuffling, and had forgotten the mechanical grace of lifting their hats from their heads as they passed over this poor threshold.

Jennie arose slowly from beside the white sheeted form and walked wearily to the window; her face was white and drawn, but tearless. How could she weep that the weary life was ended in

" Let not your heart be troubled."—Page 203.

infinite rest? She could almost rejoice with the
released spirit. She tried to follow it to the
Paradise of God, but poor Jennie's theological
views were sadly obscure; while she was sure
that her mother had gone to Heaven, she herself
seemed only more surely barred out, and she was
beginning to have a dreadful, listless feeling that
it did not matter much what became of her, and
to feel rather sure she had been lost from the
beginning, as though God could, after giving His
Son for a ransomed world, let any soul be eter-
nally lost.

Some one touched her rudely on the shoulder.
It was the undertaker's man ; but when she
turned, and he saw her face, he stepped back and
touched his hat.

"It's all right now," he said, with a glance of
professional inspection toward the coffin. "It's
snug and light, quite fit for a lady. And here's
the bill, Miss."

Jennie took the slip of paper and paid the
amount it called for with her last poor earnings.
The man still lingered, and looked appealingly
toward Mrs. Lannigan, the woman from whom
Jennie rented the rooms.

"It 's the funeral he manes," said that person, coming forward. "As ye refused to have any wake, perhaps ye won't mind hevin' any praste or funeral, Miss."

"No," said Jennie, hoarsely; "there will be no funeral ; you can send here this afternoon, for the — the body. That is all."

The man was accustomed to straits of all kinds, in life and in death; it did not matter whether the clay was coarse and common, or lovely and refined; to get it out of the way as speedily as possible was his sole object. But here was something he did not like to encounter, this white, fixed despair of the living. He tried to think of something consoling to say, and finally remarked:

"If it would make you feel any better, Miss, there 's a minister lives down by the Lake, who would come willingly, and say a prayer or two at the time of the fun'ral. He 's a mighty nice sort of man, and does n't belong to any particular church; but is a real, wide-awake Christian, on a pretty big scale."

"Holy Mother! he manes the man that praches in the theaytre," ejaculated Mrs. Lannigan.

"That's because no other place will hold the people who go to hear him. He's what they call a sympathetic preacher, and makes every one feel as if he'd been as sinful and as miserable as they are. He will do you good, Miss, if any one can."

"Thank you," answered Jennie, passively; "perhaps he would not care to come; but if he will, he may at least offer a prayer, not for the dead but for the living."

She had heard this preacher, absorbed as she had at the time been, in sinful pleasures and an unholy love; she had never forgotten his words, but she remembered him as popular, gifted, and prosperous. Would he condescend to visit poverty and sin?

He came that afternoon; a slight, dark man, with a pleasant face and a wonderful magnetism of manner. Jennie was bending over the thin, white face of her mother, taking that final agonized look that must last the hungry heart so long — so long, when a hand, tender and kindly as a woman's, fell upon her head, and a low, persuasive voice said:

"Let not your heart be troubled; ye believe in God, believe also in Me."

She stood erect, calmed, hushed, by that low, controlling voice. Reverently the minister approached the dead, and gazed for a moment in silence; then he looked about the room. There were present, the undertaker's men, Mrs. Lannigan — her prejudices revealed in her face — two or three dirty, slatternly women, who had dropped in, and looked half-sober, half-aggressive and wholly incongruous, and the tall, slender, beautiful girl, with the manners of a lady, the plain black dress of a nun, and a face of desolate anguish. Then he bowed his head in prayer.

I wish I could reproduce his words here; but the fire on the altar is dead. They did their work, however. Jennie felt a peace, such as she had never before known, steal over her soul; Mrs. Lannigan forgot the man was not "a praste," and cried aloud ; while every heart there was touched as by a divine influence.

After the prayer the minister talked to them. It was not prayer, it was not preaching, just a few comforting texts, a revelation of God as the Father, instead of the Judge.

"Man," he said, "had come to us in all ages, and offered us a Deity fashioned after the nearest

king or despot, and millions of children, old and
young, have gone to bed at night, whispering
their prayers to a Deity, not so kind, nor so
sweet, nor so just, as the mother who had just
bidden them 'good night.' In past days there
used to be a dreadful fear that perhaps we might
any night go from the kingdom of our mother
to the kingdom of God. Our mother seemed
always more beautiful than such a God. Now
we know Him as He is, long suffering and
patient, tender, and of infinite compassion, ready
to hear and to save; the friend of sinners."

Then he turned to Jennie, with the words,
"Your mother has bidden you good night, and
gone to her rest; in the sunshine of eternal day,
you will bid her a blessed good morning. Remember that 'whosoever will' may find Him;
the golden chords of love are ever drawing us
upward into the atmosphere of rest, peace, and
compensation, where He dwells. Christ died for
us, God lives for us, for you and me. Trust
Him; no matter how often you fail and faint,
fall or stumble, feel in the dark for His hand,
and it will lead you out of great darkness into
perfect light."

" Sure he spakes as well as any praste I ever heard," said Mrs. Lannigan, wiping her eyes and shuffling out of the room after. the bearers and the coffin, leaving Jennie alone to the desolation of a dwelling vacated by death.

The minister shook hands with her and went 'his way. He had treated her just as he would have treated any other sorrowing human soul, irrespective of surroundings. He knew she was under the ban of sin, but what particular sin he did not ask nor care to know; he came to her as a messenger from God, bringing glad tidings of great joy, if she would but receive them.

That night a reaction set in, and Jennie raved with fever. Mrs. Lannigan and her set did what they could, for the Irish heart has a fountain of kindness down in its depths. Those poor scrub-women took care of Jennie as well as they knew how, and when she arose, like a ghost, from that sick-bed, they tried to find work for her.

Did you ever try to find work in a large city, where the supply of laborers constantly exceeds the demand? If you are a woman, young, deli-cate, and without friends, you will find the battle a tough one. There are thousands of such cases

in this great city, of women, young, weak, and
helpless, who have drifted here from the green
fields of the country, and fought the demon of
want, toil, and hardship, till they went down and
were lost to sight forever.   There is no Young
Women's Christian Association.

The homes of the rich open their doors wide
to the Ross Farnhams of society, but they are
shut and barred to his victim.   Very good.   The
way of the transgressor should be hard.   But
what about those who have not yet become trans-
gressors; who are hesitating over the fatal plunge?
They should not be dependent upon the caprices
of one woman or many.   An association of the
strongest and best women in the city, women
above petty, personal feelings, above the strife of
party preferment, and influenced by the divine
principles of humanity, should be formed to
warn, help, and save, not the fallen, but the
falling; not to tell the story with illustrations at
every social gathering, but to do so much, that
there will not be a story to tell; to supplement
every saving deed with another, till they reach
the skies.   The church cannot do this work,

neither can the State; it is for loyal Christian womanhood to accomplish.

The next chapter in Jennie's true story may sound like a burlesque; it is but a faithful transcription of what actually occurred at a veritable meeting. It is not intended to cast any slur upon the public conventions of women, but there are good people who will readily testify to the faithfulness of the report.

CHAPTER XXIV.

IN SOLEMN CONCLAVE.

THERE was a meeting of the B. W. A. Society in one of the public halls of the city. Notices had appeared in the evening and morning papers, announcing it, stating that it was to be held in the interests of reform, and calling upon all thinking women to come forward and endorse it by their presence. The afternoon named found a large audience, composed of women, prominent in all public work; women who seldom went anywhere but to church; literary women, business women, and fashionable women; with also a number of earnest, thinking women, who seldom found time to attend such a gathering, but hoped for much good from this. There was also a sprinkling of men, reformers, free-thinkers, lawyers, and politicians. They all looked curious and uncomfortable, as though they did not know what they were there for.

A very pretty woman, in green silk, point lace, and diamonds, sat with the other women on the platform, and nodded and smiled approvingly as one and another she had invited to be present, came in. This was the Hon. Mrs. Bliss, who was a leader in society, as well as an enthusiastic member of the B. W. A. S. Having never worked any herself, she felt called upon to advocate the cause of working women. Her soft complexion and tranquil features seemed cast in the mould of an eternal smile — simper, her enemies called it; however, she made a charming centrepiece for the platform, and when she clasped her hands in mimic feeling the diamonds sparkled beautifully.

The meeting was called to order by the President of the Society, Mrs. Monroe, who made a brief address, announcing that it was strictly a women's meeting, and would the gentlemen please to withdraw?

Upon this about a dozen arose, looked very much abashed, and filed out noiselessly, as if afraid of waking somebody. The doors were closed, and the President was about to proceed to business, when she discovered a young man busily sharpening a pencil. His pink cheeks were dimpling with professional mirth as he imagined he had been overlooked; but as he caught the eye of the superior officer, and saw the uplifted finger, he took his hat and meekly retired with the rest, and once more peace reigned in the hall.

Then the President gave her address. The magnetism of her personal appearance, added to the air of self-conviction natural to her, inspired her followers with a devout faith in her ability to work wonders. That she never did accomplish anything was left for the records to show. She had the faculty of talking well, and filling the air with the small shot of sounding ideas, which never killed any wrong. Her hobby now, was to reclaim the fallen, and she unrolled a petition that looked like a panorama of Egypt, and requested every lady present to sign it. There were models of hospitals, asylums, refuges, co-operative boarding-houses, foundling homes, and what not, covering one side of it. The opposite side held the petitioners' names.

The majority of the ladies were delighted with the drawings. A community on paper looks so well; but they did not care to add their names just yet. A few appended straggling signatures, and felt as if they were signing a new Emancipation document.

When Mrs. Monroe sat down, a modest looking woman, in a quiet suit of gray, with white hair banded back under a Quaker's bonnet, arose and said:

"It seems to me it would be a pleasant and kindly thing to prevent those women from the necessity of falling. If thee would make more familiar acquaintance with these young working girls, and hedge them about with social companionship of their own kind, and help them to the innocent pleasures of life, thee would help them to preserve their purity, and I hold that would be better than wading into a pit to help them out."

"I second that," said an earnest voice from the gallery; "especially if we have helped dig the pit, as so many of us have, into which they are fallen."

"And I claim that it is easier to save ten girls from falling, than to reform one who has fallen," added another.

"That is not the object of this meeting," said the President. "It is the sick who need a physician. I—"

"Mrs. President," shrieked an old lady, with a very high forehead and a sanctimonious whine, "I think I perceive a man in the gallery!"

Had she announced the presence of a royal Bengal tiger it could not have produced a more decided sensation. Though nothing had been said, or was likely to be said, that might not be spoken upon the house-top, the air of mystery that enveloped the meeting made it presumable that something dreadful was coming. At this announcement one-half of the audience sprang to their feet in alarm, and everybody stared at the gallery. The man proved to be a very comely young woman, in a reform dress, and she was at once invited to a seat on the platform.

The next speaker was a benevolent-looking, elderly woman, who wished to present a special case.

"It is that of a young girl," she said, "who came here from the country and lived with some woman — she did not give me her name — who betrayed her in the basest manner. She was totally ignorant of the ways of the world, a mere child in years, and the only child of poor parents, who expected much from her. She was betrayed by this woman into the hands of a libertine relative who had been cared for under her father's poor roof; the man did not cast her off, but it would have come to the same thing in the end. He deluded her for awhile with the old sophistry, about mere formalities, and as she was extremely beautiful, he maintained her in magnificence.

"The awakening came when she found her old mother wandering about the streets, in rags and insanity, looking for her lost child, and learned that her father had died by his own hand upon hearing of her disgrace. She took her mother to poor lodgings, resigned all that her lover. had bestowed upon her, and went to work to make an honest living. After a dreadful struggle, during which no friend she had ever known before would speak to her, her mother died, and she herself has just risen from a bed of sickness, where she was nursed and tended by some common laboring people — poor in all but kindness. .

" I know there are ladies here to-day who can

assure this girl's future by giving her employment; she can sew beautifully and do all kinds
of embroidery, but she is not strong enough to
do housework. She says that she was a sort of
companion to the woman who first brought her
to this city; some of you who have invalid friends
might find her useful in that way. I would take
her myself, but I expect to leave the city in a
few days, for Europe. She promised to come
here this afternoon, and here she is," added the
speaker as the door opened and shut, and a slight,
fair girl entered and sat down near the entrance,
as if hiding from observation.

Mrs. Monroe was very much agitated by the
appearance of this girl; but no one noticed her,
for all eyes were turned upon the slender figure
in black, while a murmur of admiring comment
ran through the assembly. How beautiful she
was! Her skin was almost transparent in its
delicacy; her large, dark eyes were sad and wistful, and her features were exquisitely regular.
The expression of her face was that of one who
has suffered much, and the large, dark eyes —
larger and darker from sickness — were fixed
with imploring intensity upon her one friend

present — the lady who was presenting her case. Need I say that this girl was Jennie Armstrong!

When Jennie looked up and saw Mrs. Monroe it seemed to her as if she must turn and fly, if even into great darkness. The woman who had so treacherously befriended her; who had been bribed, as she now believed, to betray her!

The ladies crowded about her, and asked a multitude of questions, some of which brought the hot flush of sensibility to her cheeks. They meant it kindly enough, and intended to try and help her; but there seemed to be no decision of purpose. Each one felt obliged to ask permission . of her husband, or of some relative, before she could give the stranger a home. One lady, a prominent member of a then prominent church, offered to consult her minister, and abide by his decision; she was a pretty, vain, impulsive woman, who did about as she pleased, making liberal donations to the church, giving fine presents to the minister's wife, and wearing larger diamonds and more of them than any member of her society. She made up in appearance what she lacked in intelligence, and the Church smiled at her follies and did good with her money. She had come here to-day out of respect for Mrs. Bliss, and she felt really grieved for the young girl who looked so sorrow-stricken; she summed up in her own mind the cast-off dresses she would bestow upon her, and she was sure the Church would act handsomely in the matter.

Mrs. Monroe felt that she must say something. It was expected of her; but all the bitterness of her nature seemed to surge up and choke her. One lady, who had been regarding her fixedly, and had noted her agitation, now said:

"Perhaps, Mrs. President, you know something of this case, and will advise us what to do with the girl."

There is no cruelty so malignant as that of a small nature. Mrs. Monroe had much at stake; it had been her intention, from the moment Jennie entered, not to take any step toward acknowledging a past acquaintance; that she felt might not be creditable to herself in all eyes. Now that she was called upon and must speak, she chose to say:

"I know her to be confirmed in ways of sin."

It was the one blow too much. Perhaps she thought Jennie would not dare resent it. The girl sprang to her feet and walked up the aisle, with flashing eyes, and confronted the speaker. In these years she had learned to speak with dignity and clearness. The reformer sank back in her chair, and her features assumed an air of stony defiance.

'How dare you insult me so!" cried the girl, looking at her as if, in her frenzy, she might spring upon her. "I may be bad — I certainly have been — but I am a thousand times better than you! What is your marriage to you, but a lie — but perjury! I have not murdered the innocent, as you have done! I have never turned helpless girls into the streets, to further a base purpose, and then taunted them with the sin I helped them to commit! *You* help the fallen! *You* lead people to a higher life! I tell you, it is you, and such as you, that bring discredit on the charities of better women! If I were home-less, houseless, and starving — as God knows I am — I would never touch the bread that you offered me, or sleep under a roof that your charity had procured me!"

She was whiter than any dead woman when she sat down, mentally and physically exhausted. A suppressed murmur ran through the hall, met by severe tokens of displeasure from the adherents of Mrs. Monroe, who rallied about her in vehement indignation. Cries of "Shame! shame to attack such a good woman!" "Turn her into the streets again; she is totally depraved," etc., etc., rung through the hall.

The lady who had brought Jennie there came to her at once, accompanied by the pretty friend of Mrs. Bliss. This was Mrs. Bailey, who had made up her elaborate mind to take a step without consulting the minister, and as she was going to the watering places for the season, to give Jennie a home in consideration of certain duties in connection with her summer wardrobe. Jennie parted with her friend of a few weeks with genuine sorrow.

CHAPTER XXV.

MRS. GRUNDY AND FATE.

NOW indeed, Providence seemed to befriend Jennie. Mrs. Bailey proved to be very kind in her way, demanding but light service of her, and was always pleasant and considerate. She knew just what Jennie's past history had been, and was inclined to lay all the blame where it justly belonged; but on this portion of her life Jennie was mute, and Mrs. Bailey had tact enough to let it alone. She was rather fond of a foolish, good-looking husband, who believed everything she told him, no matter how improbable, and she liked all other gentlemen well enough to flirt vigorously with them upon all possible occasions. Whatever entanglements she got into she came out of with flying colors, helped by the infantile innocence of her face and the endorsement of the Church. She was very much in love with life, and the world, which had used her well.

"I hope you are comfortable," she said, looking in upon Jennie, the first day of her engagement. "This is the coolest room in the house; but I daresay you find it warm sewing. I think you may rip off all the lace upon that pink silk; I have several yards of new point to trim it with, and you will find the buttons in my workbasket; they were fifteen dollars a dozen, and are perfectly lovely. When you finish that, you may do the knife plaiting for that violet organdie. I shall be out an hour or more."

When she was left alone, Jennie threw down her work and began a slow walk up and down the room. The work was utterly and wholly distasteful to her, and a dreadful weariness seemed to have taken possession of her, much of which was due to ill health. Would she never be well again, and strong enough to work with comfort? She walked to the elegant mirror shrouded in costly lace, and looked at herself. Heavens! how like a penitent she looked, in her coarse black dress. She held up her hands; how white and thin they were! A ring she wore —

her mother's wedding ring — just a small, worn circlet of gold, nearly dropped off her finger.

This sort of life, with its hardships and sneers and snubs, was wearing her out; but she had an inner consciousness that she was doing right; she had tried to be true to herself. She would live down that short and fatal past, that had branded her with infamy. She went back to her sewing, and worked to make up for lost time. She sewed till her back ached and her face flushed, and it was very hard to breathe; and still she sewed on.

"Why not?" she thought, bitterly. "Better women do it every day, and who pities or cares for them!"

A few days after this, when Mrs. Bailey was absent on one of her frequent shopping excursions, her brother from the North Side came in, and, as he was accustomed to do, went through the house, looking for his sister, seeking her, at last, in the front room up-stairs where Jennie was sewing. He was a bachelor, the eldest of the family, and a man who had seen the world in all its phases. He was so sure of finding his sister in her favorite room that he walked in without ceremony, before he saw that a stranger occupied it.

"Excuse me, Miss," he said, bowing carelessly, "but I expected to find Mrs. Bailey here." Then he stared blankly at Jennie's flushed face, ejaculated, "The devil!" and went out, slamming the door behind him.

At the front gate he met his sister, coming in. "Alice, who is that girl?" he asked, pointing up-stairs.

Mrs. Bailey had just bought a Chantilly lace fichu at a bargain, consequently she was in radiant good humor.

"Who is — that — girl?" she repeated slowly. "Why, she is a seamstress furnished me by a Society in the city; she sews beautifully. Isn't she handsome?"

"Well, yes, rather. I should keep Tom out of her way; you know how susceptible he is."

"Why, you dreadful boy! My Tom! Why, I don't believe he could tell whether she is white or copper-colored. Now with you it would be entirely different."

"Humph! yes, I think it would. By the way, 'Alice, when did you see Ross Farnham last?"

"When! why at the last reception; I danced with him. He dances elegantly; but then he is an elegant gentleman." And she smiled innocently into her brother's face.

"Well, you need not fall down and worship him, if he is. Ross is well enough as we fellows go, but his reputation is beginning to be a little shaky, even with us, and you know that means a great deal. Tom is such a good fellow he never knows any harm of anybody; but I won't see my sister imposed on by any one with a character like Ross Farnham's."

"Thanks, dear; your sister appreciates your good intentions, but you know I meet many such men in society, and must be agreeable to them. We ladies are not supposed to know of their little peccadilloes."

"There you are mistaken, Alice. Such men are not common; society men are not all unprincipled *roues*, and even among them Ross Farnham is despised."

"Yet I hear he is going to marry that pretty and accomplished Miss Badger, an only daughter and an heiress."

"Certainly; you ladies always exalt such a

man into a hero. To be a libertine or a brigand is sure to make a man successful in laying siege to your hearts."

"Nonsense, Frank; you are jealous. You know you were in love with Ida Badger yourself — all the gentlemen are," retorted his sister.

"Perhaps. Well, she had the bad taste to select Ross, and I surrender gracefully. Good bye, Alice, I'm off." And he walked away, humming a lively air.

At the first corner he stopped and looked back. "It isn't just the thing for Alice to have that girl in the house; I wonder if she knows anything about her. How cut up the poor thing looks! I wonder if Farnham does anything for her; it is rough, I must say. I will think about it before I speak to Alice."

"I wonder how long it will be before she will come up and say I am not wanted," thought Jennie, who knew how vacillating Mrs. Bailey could be at times.

It seemed now as if there might be a respite for the poor girl from the fate that faced her; but the second week of her engagement brought a social morning call from a wealthy member of

15

the Church, who was a dragon of virtue herself, and tolerated no lapses of it in others. She had been present at the meeting of the Society when Jennie made her brief speech, and she had taken sides with Mrs. Monroe, and heard that lady's version of Jennie's baseness and ingratitude. Mrs. Bailey, who had no idea of this being a special visit, called to the girl to·show Mrs. Holton up-stairs, and in a few moments the visitor entered the sewing-room, very hot and flushed, and exceedingly pompous.

Mrs. Bailey hastened to bring forward the coolest and most comfortable chair in the room, and her caller was just about to settle herself in it, when her cold, gray eyes lighted on Jennie, sewing meekly, without even raising her head. There was instantly a storm of indignant protestation, as Mrs. Holton appealed to Mrs. Bailey to know if this was an intentional insult.

·"That girl!" shrieked Mrs. Holton, looking in imminent danger of apoplexy. "Do you know who she is, and then bring me — me — into the very same room with her!"

"Dear Mrs. Holton!" gasped Mrs. Bailey; for this was a Church pillar, worth half a million.

"Forgive me; but indeed I never thought of
her. You know I employed her purely from
charity; she had no home, and is such a lovely
hand to make over — and — and, do you really
think that she is wicked now?"

"Wicked! Steeped in wickedness."

Poor Jennie had escaped from the room by
this time, and Mrs. Holton had fallen back
in the rocking-chair, and was fanning herself
violently.

"Of course, you can have no conception of
what she is; but you wrong yourself and society
by keeping such a creature under your roof.
And last Sunday you took her to church, and
actually allowed her to sit in your pew; and my
son — *my* son, Mrs. Bailey — saw her, and no
doubt thought she was a relative of yours. He
said she had an interesting face, and he felt sure
she had a history. A history, indeed! I should
think she had."

Here the woman stopped for want of breath,
and Mrs. Bailey, who was really kind-hearted,
ventured another appeal for Jennie.

"She was so young, Mrs. Holton, and she had
no friends here, and her punishment has been so

dreadful. Can we not do something for her, amongst us?"

"Certainly," responded the matron, with great dignity; "there is the Refuge and the Good Shepherd, institutions for just such cases. I myself will recommend her as a suitable applicant."

If Mrs. Bailey had been a woman of spirit she would, at this moment, have turned the Hon. Mrs. Holton out of her house, and remanded Jennie back to her work; but she was bound, hand and foot, by the golden chains of conservatism, and she was loyal to her tyrant. So she meekly said:

"She would not live a week in either place; but she might get work where they did not know about her past life."

"Well, I have done my duty as Directress of our Society. If you continue to harbor this girl under your roof we shall feel it to be our duty as mothers and consistent church members, to keep our young people from all contact with her, and you will find, dear Mrs. Bailey, your own position a very unpleasant one."

"I am going away in a week," said Mrs.

Bailey, who anticipated her departure, in hopes of conciliating her mentor, "and shall have no further need of her services. She has behaved well since she has been here, and done her work faithfully; but perhaps it is better as you say — the influence may be wrong. I shall, of course, act upon your advice, and am greatly obliged."

She closed the front door, as her visitor sailed majestically down the steps, and went back to find Jennie. She discovered her in the small bedroom allotted to her use, thrown face downward upon the bed, crying bitterly.

"Isn't it a shame!" exclaimed Mrs. Bailey. "Of course you heard every word she said; that horrid woman! But we all have to do just as she says. Now, what will you do?"

"Oh," said Jennie, sitting up and wiping the tears from her drenched face, "I must look for another situation, of course; I do not expect to stay here. You have been very kind to me. It is very hard, living in this way with no friends of my own, and I am so, so wretched." And Jennie began to sob again.

"I tell you what," began Mrs. Bailey, as a sudden thought took possession of her; "go and see our minister. He is a beautiful man; such white hands, and so consoling! If any one can help you he can, and he is very benevolent. I will see him to-night, at prayer meeting, and say that you will be there to-morrow evening; he will be at his study in the church then. I am so glad I thought of him. Now, will you go?"

"Yes," said Jennie, whose soul still found comfort in the echoes of that other minister's words of comfort, "I will go."

CHAPTER XXVI.

THE GOSPEL OF GUSH.

T was a beautiful church, and the minister was a beautiful man! Handsome to look at and good to listen to; his voice was soft and persuasive, and had an undertone of gospel sweetness. He stood in the door of his fold, and called his sheep gently and they came gladly at their shepherd's call. It was so easy to follow him and obey his commands. He was not a wolf in sheep's clothing, either, but a kind, considerate pastor, who had prayed and pleaded with his people, always in that same gentle voice, and with that sweet, persuasive manner, until he had lost his strength, amassed a fortune, and shifted half the burden of securing the salvation of souls on other shoulders. The ladies of his congregation adored him. They heaped upon him embroidered slippers and quilted silk dressing gowns, and poured out all the secret sorrows of their hearts into the confessional of his gentle ears. When he made his ministerial calls, Mrs. A. told him how she hated Mrs. B., and he cast oil on the troubled waters. When his health failed he met his people in his study at the church.

Here Jennie sought him. Her courage nearly failed her when she stood in the door-way, but she felt that if ever a poor, sinful mortal needed help she was that one; so she tapped lightly on the study door, and waited with a fearful heart. She was thankful that he knew she was coming, and would have thought over her needs beforehand, and be ready to throw some light on her dark, shadowed path.

In response to her timid knock he opened the door, and she saw that he was alone. He extended his hand — such a beautiful hand, soft, white, and supple — and smiled kindly, all the while looking over her shoulder in a nervous, frightened manner, into the church corridor beyond, feebly lighted by a dim lamp. As soon as she entered he locked the door, and in answer to Jennie's look of surprise, said:

"I do not wish to be interrupted. There is a choir meeting in the church to-night, and if any of the members saw you come in there would be a dozen excuses. made to get in here. Now, if you please, I am ready to hear your story."

"My story!" echoed Jennie, surprised and hurt; "I thought you knew it; that Mrs. Bailey had told you."

He smiled pleasantly. "Mrs. Bailey is so romantic, and so much the creature of feeling, that I always find it impossible to discriminate between the real and the imaginary in her stories. If you will give me an outline of your life I will see what can be done for you."

She told him all, trying to forget that it was anything else but soul talking to soul; yet she lacked the inspiration which his presence should have given her. This emissary of our Blessed Master had neither sinned nor suffered; his face was smooth and seamless; no indentures from the crown of thorns had given character to his brow; no stormy surges of feeling had paled his cheek. How could he appreciate this girl's temptation and sorrow! How could he sympathize with the anguish that oppressed her!

He heard her through kindly, listening with passive emotion to the whole sad story of her temptation and fall, the death of her father and mother, her own repentance, and the world's scorn. He was accustomed to gushing confidences of sin and folly, while a jeweled white hand would be laid softly upon his shoulder to emphasize the story, and a sparkling shower of repentant tears would follow, and the next day a check for the dear pastor to use toward some favorite project. But this poorly-clad, sorrowing girl was of another sort. She had a fineness of organization that would offer a life of atonement for a year of sin. How should he deal with one who was so different from the lambs of his own flock!

A ray of light reached the perplexed pastor. It came from the key-hole of the study door. He rose nervously and hung his handkerchief over the knob. As he did so there was a sudden rustling without.

"There was a member of the choir on her knees there," he said, looking very nervous and uncomfortable. "Do you think any one saw you come in?"

"And if any one did," answered Jennie, with a shade of contempt in her voice, "what of it? Surely my presence in your study cannot hurt you, sir!"

"No-o," was the cautious reply; "but if my wife came in she might be angry, and those other women; oh dear! you cannot understand; but they are ready to tear me in pieces between them, and if they saw you here, I should probably be blamed for not calling a church council in the matter. No, I really cannot help you without making matters worse. I have so many similar cases presented to my notice that, were I to give attention to them all, I should have no time left to do my Blessed Master's work. Try and live a better life; remember that Christ died for sinners, such as you, and — and — are you going? Do not let any one see you if you can help it."

Such were the husks he offered to her starving soul.

The good pastor did not feel quite satisfied with himself, however, and the next day he called on Ross Farnham, at his elegant hotel, to remonstrate with him upon his sin, and to ask him to do something for Jennie. When informed that she would neither see Ross nor receive aid from him, the minister felt that he was released from further interest in the matter, and sat down to a luxurious dinner, as Mr. Farnham's guest, with a clear conscience and a good digestion.

On the event of the pastor's birth-day, a few weeks later, a superb silver-mounted dressing-case was sent in, with Ross Farnham's compliments!

Verily, the laborer is worthy of his hire!

CHAPTER XXVII.

VIRTUE PROTECTED.

SIN is sweet! Whatever bitterness it may leave at the last, its first taste is sugared to the palate. It is not till the draught reaches the soul, and strikes its deadly blight there, that the victim feels it is a fearful poison. All the ways to sin are made alluring—bright with pleasure, blooming with light, and full of gay company. The narrow path is hard to walk in: It is full of self-denial; the brambles cut and tear the fainting flesh; the jeers of those who are going the other way make a constant din; but at the end are the Eternal Heights, and to him that overcometh it shall be given to be a pillar in the temple of God. I have always thought that passage should read to *her* that overcometh, since it is woman alone who must walk in the prescribed path.

Upon this narrow path Jennie had entered, weary, hungry, sorrowful, and alone.

Where was Reuben all this time? Back again at the hospital, wearing out, in the struggle for breath. He lost all trace of Jennie when she left Mrs. Lannigan's. At last he wrote to Eva Bartlett, asking her to help him find her, and Eva gladly went to work to make a home for Jennie, and wrote her views of the matter to Reuben. It was then decided, that upon his death, which was certain at no very distant time, and might occur at any moment, that Jennie should live with Mrs. Harlow, on the old place, and take charge of his mother during her lifetime, if she would. In any case, half of his estate was willed to her, that she might not want. Yet all this time the poor girl had not where to lay her head.

At last another chance among the great whirlpool of bread-seekers drifted within her reach. She answered an advertisement for a seamstress, and was taken upon trust with scarcely a question asked her. This was not from any Christ-like goodness of heart in the people who employed her. To them, a seamstress was a mere machine who came from somewhere in the back regions of the city at seven o'clock in the morning, sewed all day, and disappeared into the same remote and shadowy distance after six at night. Good, bad, or indifferent in morals, it made no difference to them. If any of them had thought about it at all, they would have decided that she would naturally be bad. Somehow that seemed to be most likely, yet if the fingers were deft, and did their work well, all right. The soul might be as black as ink, so long as none of the color rubbed off on the work.

Jennie's new employer was Mrs. Colonel Badger, a lady of unquestioned position in society. Her only daughter was about to marry a gentleman of great wealth, considerably older than herself.

"I don't love him one bit," said the gay creature, chatting to a young friend in the sewing room, while she waited for measures to be taken and patterns adjusted.

"Then why do you marry him, Ida?" asked her less wordly friend.

"Because he is so splendid and stylish, and all the girls want him. And think of the diamonds

I shall have.   And we are going to Europe on a bridal tour, and will stay there until we are tired of it.   And he is so fond of me!"

"Reasons enough!   Why has he never married before?   He is quite an old bachelor," said her friend.

"He never loved before," was the triumphant answer.   "He has confessed all his sins to me, and is going to join the church — our church, you know — and live a new life.   He's been a pretty gay boy, I can tell you, but I will take care of him now."

Amid such chatter as this, Jennie sat and sewed, listened, and wondered if Heaven would bless such an ill-assorted union as this.   Apparantly, it did.

She earned her bread here.   The bride-elect was haughty and shrewish, and berated her mother, the servants, and the seamstress.   At night, when Jennie went down the stairs, she would feel numb with repressed misery, and the long lonely walk to Mrs. Lannigan's — for she was again a lodger under that humble roof — was beset with peril.   The temptations — sometimes horrible and grotesque, sometimes sugared and engaging — which come to young and beautiful women who go along the streets unprotected, followed her to the threshold of her poor home. Once a spectral figure glided up to peer into her face.

. Jennie remembered her. It was the woman who had watched her upon the night of her arrival in the city. The tawdry, painted creature who had flitted athwart her vision like a warning, was dressed then in gorgeous silk, and now she was in rags, her beauty and grace gone with her diamonds to keep her from starving.

"I knew it," she chuckled. "He tired of you, just as he did of me — of them all. Oh, it's a bonny sight — ha! ha! Look here!" She held up two skeleton arms, and then, with a wild scream, flitted away into the darkness.

One evening there came over her such a dreadful loneliness, such a longing for human help and sympathy, that she ventured to go and call on Lucia Winne, to learn something of Reuben, of Eva, and the rest. She bent her steps toward Lucia's boarding place, and in a short time was following a servant to her room. It was a pretty place, filled with light and bloom, and

16

Lucia was seated cosily at a table writing. She turned as the girl announced a caller.

"Jennie!" she exclaimed; the name passed her lips before she could stop it, and she immediately added, "How dared you come here? What would my brother say?"

"I wanted to see you, Lucia, to let you know I am living right now, and have been for a long time. Can you never forget nor forgive?" asked the poor girl, wildly.

"You should have thought of that before," answered Lucia, in an icy tone. "You had the same chance Eva and I had, Jennie, but you willfully chose to do wrong, and you ought to suffer. I can never associate with you again. I cannot help you up without pulling myself down."

"If you had suffered what I have," returned Jennie —"cold, hunger, shame, and scorn — you might think I was sufficiently punished, Lucia, for the disgrace I brought upon those who loved and trusted me. But, Lucia, my mother forgave me with her last breath. I have never injured you. Surely, you can forget my past."

"I cannot, Jennie, so do not ask it. If you

are indeed penitent, I am glad, but your life must prove it. Oh, Jennie! have you thought what it is to die?"

"No," answered Jennie, wearily. "It takes all my time to try to live, and live right. When such great good luck as dying comes to me, my troubles and necessities will be over."

"Repent while there is yet time," said Lucia. "I know some good people who will remember you in their prayers."

Jennie smiled drearily. "It might hurt the purity of their souls to pray for me," she replied. "Good bye, Lucia. There is a great gulf between us. Be thankful you have not crossed it." She held out her hand, but Lucia did not see it, and so they parted, in this life, forever!

She had several panics of fright while sewing at the Badger's. It was part of her punishment that her beauty and Ross Farnham's wealth and position should have made her conspicuously known, and she dreaded the entrance of any friend who might by chance recognize her. One day a vivacious young lady called, who was a great friend of the bride-elect, and was

at once taken into the room where Jennie and
the others were sewing, to inspect the bridal
finery. It happened that she was a distant relative of Mr. Monroe, and a cordial hater of Mrs.
Monroe, as she was of all shams. She was a
shrewd, sensible Scotch girl, who had made a
flattering success with her pen, and was quite
the fashion in society. Agnes McDonald knew
the pale seamstress the moment she saw her, but
by no word nor look did she betray the knowledge. At a moment when they were left alone
together, for Agnes stayed to lunch, Jennie
threw down the work she was vainly trying to
finish, and, clasping her hands in passionate
entreaty, looked into the honest kindly face.

"Oh, Miss McDonald, please do not say that
you ever saw me before, nor betray anything
about my past life. These people do not know
or care anything about me, but if they did know,
I might be without a situation again; and I
must have bread!"

"Dinna ye fash yoursel," said Agnes McDonald, coolly. "If they never find out till they
learn it frae me, they'll bide a weary while.
And it's little they're likely to ken at the last.

And as for your sin — we 're all truly sinners, more or less. Just ye put it behind ye till ye 're asked for it at the Last Day! Dinna ye fash about it any mair."

Homely words, but so comforting. Jennie smiled into the honest, kindly face with her eyes full of tears, and stitched on the rest of that day with a lighter heart, for the few kind words that had been given her.

Jennie's dark spectre of fate was again nearing her. It was strange that not once during the weeks she worked there was the name of Ida Badger's affianced husband spoken in her presence. It was the merest chance, as his visits were almost daily, but the rooms used for sewing were in a remote part of the large house, and the conversation carried on there was chiefly of the wardrobe. If she had pictured him at all in her mind, it was as an elderly man of rather imposing appearance. The pet abbreviation by which his lady-love mentioned him meant little or nothing to her.

One evening as Jennie came down the stairs into the spacious hall, on her way to the side door, by which she always came and went, she

found the upper housemaid hurriedly lighting
the hall lamp. The gas was turned off, or was
obstinate, and she was perplexed with it, while a
vigorous ring at the front door was still unan-
swered. "Would ye mind opening the door,
Miss?" she asked, regulating the flame in the
frosted glass globe. "It's Miss Ida's gentleman, and he don't like to be kept waiting."

Jennie opened the door, and stepped back to
admit the gentleman. As he entered, the soft
light fell upon his face, and she gave a stifled
cry. It was Ross Farnham!

He caught her arm fiercely, as he saw who it
was, and with white, set lips looked sternly into
her death-stricken face.

"What are you doing in this house?" he
asked, deepening the intensity of his strong grip
upon her arm, until it seemed as if the frail
bone must be crushed in his hand. "How dare
you come here?" he said, drawing her into the
vestibule beyond the curious eyes of the servant.
"Did you attempt to palm off any wretched
story upon *her?*"

Jennie looked into his handsome face. Oh,
how handsome it was, even when distorted by

anger and scorn; but she met, without flinching, the fierce gaze of his angry eyes, saying, in a calm, passionless voice, " I am in this house as a servant — a seamstress — a dependent. God knows I would not have come here if I had known I should meet you."

" Then stay away. Do you hear? Never come here again. You cannot live under the same roof with *her*, my pure, beautiful darling. Here is money — more than you can earn here. I would have given it to you before, if you had let me know where to find you. I will help you again if you need it, but never come into this house again!"

He tried to press the roll of bills into her hands, but as she drew back, released from his hold, she folded the scant black shawl she wore close about her, and passed away into the darkness.

CHAPTER XXVIII.

NOTHING BUT LEAVES!

"Dost know the olden story?
  It sounds so sweet, it sounds so sad,
Alas! they, both of them, must perish,
  For the too-much love they had."

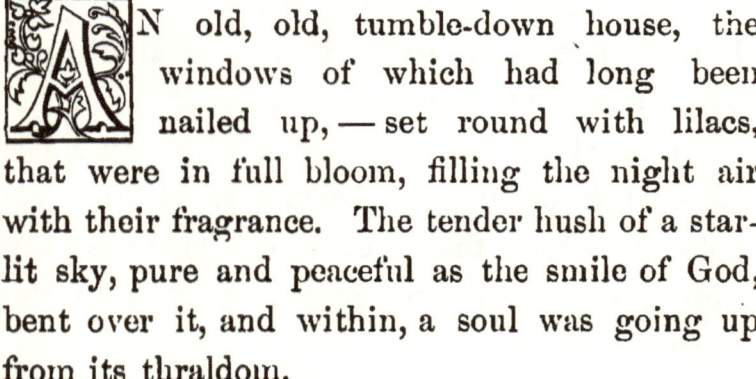N old, old, tumble-down house, the windows of which had long been nailed up, — set round with lilacs, that were in full bloom, filling the night air with their fragrance. The tender hush of a star-lit sky, pure and peaceful as the smile of God, bent over it, and within, a soul was going up from its thraldom.

She lay upon her own little bed, prepared for her by Eva's loving hands, as soon as she received poor Reuben's frantic letter, saying that he had found her, and was bringing her home!

So preternaturally long she had lain there — wasted and shadowy, with that awful immobility of feature — battling with her last enemy, all her beauty gone, and a gaunt, hollow despair in her great eyes, Ross Farnham should have seen his work then.

To what pit she had sunk; from what depths he had rescued her; what her strange or shameful experiences had been, if indeed he knew, Reuben never told. He had brought her to the old farm-house, because she babbled of it incessantly. Even now, she was murmuring snatches of song, interspersed with shrill bursts of laughter, and words of impassioned prayer.

"She has been this way ever since I found her," he said, in a low, husky voice, wiping the great drops of perspiration from his wasted face. "She imagines she is home with the old folks again, picking flowers in the field, or that she's going through some awful scenes in the city, yonder; or — or she's talking to him. Curse him! I sometimes doubt that there *is* a God, when I see such men as he live and prosper."

"Don't Reuben! It will all be right and clear as noonday to us, by and by. Poor Jennie! It is nearly over. She cannot last through the night. And we had planned so much for her!"

"This is best," said Reuben, hoarsely. "I can die contented when I know she is safe."

He burst into a violent fit of coughing, and Eva approached the sick girl on tip-toe. But there was no need of caution; she was too far gone for earthly sounds to disturb her.

"Jennie," she said, stooping gently over the dying girl, "do you know me?"

There was no answer. Jenny was surrounded by the shadowy phantoms evoked from a past that was fast leaving her forever.

"He said I would find her in the morning." She repeated it over and over. "He said no soul was ever lost!"

Reuben stooped over her, and looked into the dull face. She seemed to know him; her eyes moved ever so little, and she whispered a single word — "forgive."

For all answer, he clasped the cold hands in his, and pressed his trembling lips upon them.

The night wore on. Her breath was so cold, so cold. She murmured from time to time, "He said I would meet her in the morning!"

She was thinking of the minister, who had prayed over her mother.

About midnight she spoke again. "I am going to the city. Good bye, mother. How dim the lights in the street have grown. How cold it is. Say it again, Ross, that you love me. Oh, how tired I am. Is it morning yet?"

Yes; it was morning!

www.ingramcontent.com/pod-product-compliance
Lightning Source LLC
Chambersburg PA
CBHW030642030726
47497CB00006B/1904